Another Sky

Colm O'Gaora was born in Dublin in 1966. His short stories have been widely published and broadcast and were collected in *Giving Ground* (1993). His first novel, *A Crooked Field*, was published by Picador to wide acclaim in 1999. He lives in Dubl

Also by Colm O'Gaora

Giving Ground

A Crooked Field

Another Sky

Colm O'Gaora

Picador

First published 2003 by Picador

This edition published 2004 by Picador
an imprint of Pan Macmillan Ltd
Pan Macmillan, 20 New Wharf Road, London N1 9RR
Basingstoke and Oxford
Associated companies throughout the world
www.panmacmillan.com

ISBN 0 330 37080 4

A CIP catalogue record for this book is available from
the British Library.

Typeset by Intype London Ltd
Printed and bound in Great Britain by
Mackays of Chatham plc, Chatham, Kent

for Alison, Eoin & Niamh
and for my parents
Pádraic & Annette

I always dreamed I'd love you
I never dreamed I'd lose you
In my dreams I'm always strong

Mercury Rev, 'The Dark is Rising'

1 Portnew

Catherine's birthday was always a muted celebration, the first of February coming too soon after Christmas, the day hanging about us like lead. Each year we hoped that it would be different, that it would burst into light and colour like a seaside amusement ride cranked suddenly to life in the dead of winter.

It was never to be. Instead we handed our cards and presents to her across the breakfast table, the first murky February light smearing the window, our eyes still swollen with sleep. Catherine would smile, stretching the thin cleft in her lip, before unwrapping the watercolour set, colouring books, shoes or denim jeans we had bought for her. I can still see a plastic tea set spread out among the breakfast things, its brilliant colours all aglow on the table as we finished breakfast in silence, Catherine's birthday cards folded into a slot on the toast rack.

2 London

Today is bright and the sky has that cracked-ice colour, neither blue nor white. There are layers of cloud stacking up on the horizon: stratus and nimbostratus. We are in for a milder spell, the breeze-borne drizzle that makes me think of rush-hour crowds squeezing together under bus shelters, of streetlights blurred with wet.

It is the first of February. It is Catherine's birthday.

I teach geography in a London school that is shoehorned into a narrow plot between a grid of Victorian terraces and the Regent's Canal, into which more than a few of the school's footballs have made their way, bobbing along until they get trapped at the lock, where one of the boys can be trusted to retrieve them just as lunchtime ends. There is a commotion in the classroom behind me, the shuffle of feet and the splutter of stifled laughter.

'What,' I say, drawing a line beneath the date on the blackboard, 'are those clouds out there? Scott?' My back is still turned to them but I know that Scott will have been at the heart of things.

'Sir?'

'The clouds. What are they?'

'Er . . .'

There is a burst of whispering and then a giggle goes around the class.

'Nimbus, sir. Nimbus clouds.'

When I turn around, Scott is standing on his seat and peering out of the window, a hand held over his brow in the manner of a ship's lookout. He is trying his best not to laugh. It's a performance I've seen too often before.

'Good, Scott. Very good,' I say.

Scott smiles and looks down at his friends before snapping his heels together to make them laugh.

I wait for the laughing to die away. 'Now get down off your little stage and stick your head in your geography book and learn what those clouds really are.'

Scott scowls but gets down and all heads turn towards the blackboard, where I begin to draw cloud formations, the stick of chalk squeaking on the board, the dust falling away.

It is only with experience that I have learned to control a whole class by subduing certain elements within it, the two or three students around whom the rest rotate. I still weaken at the memory of those first months of teaching after I had qualified, a small school in the Black Country beyond Kidderminster, the children of car builders, welders, riveters, their clothes smelling of oil and galvanizing fluids. The headmaster bursting through the door and past me to draw the troublemakers from their desks and out of the door so quickly that I hadn't a chance to explain myself to him, and an emptiness in the classroom after he had gone, the pupils with their heads down, smiling. Later he would call me to his office to explain the mechanics of control, how to identify the ringleaders and isolate them with a question, the setting of a trap into which they would fall, building them up and knocking them down until they eventually learned not to challenge you.

'Make them feel humble, Fallon,' the headmaster advised, moving a stack of encyclopedias from one shelf to another, 'and they will learn to obey, if not respect, you. Otherwise, you can't teach, and that, after all, is what you're here for.'

I didn't stay long, moving to London as soon as a transfer came up, relieved to escape the headmaster, the pupils, who had already begun to undermine my belief in the value of education, and the grey and muddled town slumped on either side of the River Severn that reminded me too much of home. I don't think they missed me.

As the children copy my chalk diagrams into their books I sit at the desk and watch the cloud formations move across the sky, adrift like a regatta of becalmed yachts whose attempt to tack across the city has failed. The clouds are as white as Catherine's skin and I have seen their sail-like shapes many, many times before, stretched across the bay in Portnew, a westerly wind tugging at them.

3 Portnew

Ours was a seaside town, the grey fronts of the mean hotels and guesthouses that lined the seafront staring out at the North Atlantic, their view obscured only by wheeling seagulls and the boards of the old promenade that slipped further into the sand with every year.

The Atlantic damned the town to poor weather but still the holidaymakers came, year after year, drawn by the small Ferris wheel, the slot machines, the dodgems, their garish lights undimmed by rain that, even in mid-July, could set in for days. The railway ensured that they came, snaking out of the city in diesel-drawn vandalized carriages, spilling onto the strand and into the arcades, transforming the whole town from June to September.

On dry afternoons Catherine and I would worm our way through the rhododendrons that cloaked the embankment overlooking the railway station platform, the pink and purple velveteen petals peeling away on our skin and clothes, our bare arms and legs as white as parchment against the rich blackness of the soil and mulch. Further down the slope the rhododendrons thinned out before giving way to brambles and it was here that we would settle to watch the platform, sitting back on a discarded sleeper we had once dragged up from the foot of the embankment.

There were two trains on weekend mornings. One arrived at about half-past ten and another at midday. We rarely got there in time for the early train. Anyway we knew that it was mostly elderly visitors who took that first train, anxious to avoid the crowds, the high sun of midday, the children thronging the carriage aisles, and eager to secure the best place for the blue-striped deckchairs they hired and the folding stools they brought with them from home.

On the sunniest days the midday train was packed. Union Jacks flapped from open windows and the children pressed their noses to the glass like snails.

We would watch each train draw in and the visitors pour from the carriage doors and onto the flagstones, dragging all manner of things after them: plastic bags, flasks, paraffin stoves, outsize parasols, kitchen chairs, windbreaks, the inevitable buckets and spades. Often, when a birthday was being celebrated, a mother or grandmother would gingerly make her way down, a foil-wrapped cake held steady between both hands for fear of it being crushed.

It was always the gaggles of youngsters who pushed out first, shouting and roaring. They called for their friends, waving crude fishing rods and nets above their heads, bouncing with excitement at the expectation of the day that lay before them.

Their elders, too, had once pushed eagerly off the trains, running down to the shore, casting their spinners in vain from the same rocks and pier, before returning to the city at the end of the day, and on a last visit in their late-teens promising themselves that they would never return. Yet here they were again, leading toddlers by the hand, making for the promenade, the strand, those same rocks and the same point on the pier, seeing it all again through their children's eyes.

The gangs of young men were always last. They ambled off the train, beer cans and bottles clasped in their fists, clad in blue jeans and Linfield football shirts, their arms crazed with tattoos. They made for the bars and lounges of the small hotels that lined the seafront – the Mariner, Portnew House Hotel, the Seal's Rock, the Ulster Arms – invading the benches that overlooked the promenade. There they would whistle at the women and start up Loyalist singsongs. The hotel owner would often join in for fear of losing their custom or the best of his furniture and glassware if they turned against him.

Catherine and I watched them all, noting the familiar faces who returned almost every fine weekend and conjuring names for them: William Plaid, a check-shirted and severe-looking man with a King Billy moustache lugging a huge brown radio behind him; Miss Politely, a middle-aged widow or spinster who made a point of thanking the train driver and the station staff upon her arrival; Victor Goldsmith, an enormous man who shepherded his bird-like wife and six children along the platform, vulgar gold chains draped around his neck and hanging from his wrists. There were innumerable others, the names we gave them often forgotten from one year to the next and completely lost to me now, but I see them still, an identifying tic or foible fastened in my memory to be roused by a passer-by or fellow tube passenger, my mind desperately searching for the connection.

'I'd love to get away some day,' Catherine announced one afternoon after the platform had cleared, the clamour of voices fading towards the strand.

'What?'

'Get away, to another place altogether. Another world,' Catherine sighed.

I thought of the race to the moon, of Yuri Gagarin and Laika, the first dog in space. Soon there would be men on the moon. 'Why?' I asked.

'For the change, to see what's going on. Wouldn't you?'

There was always a gloriously limpid stillness about the station in the wake of the crowds, as if something had descended upon the place. Lying back on the swatch of grass that survived between the rhododendrons and the brambles, under filigrees of shadow cast by the hogweed that reached above our heads, it seemed impossible that she would want to be anywhere but here.

'No,' I said. 'I like it here. Look at it now.'

'But nothing happens.' She reached out and snapped a hogweed stem between her fingers.

'They're putting a great big wall around the RUC station. Haven't you seen it?' I offered as an example of the exciting things that could happen in Portnew.

'That's nothing, Michael,' Catherine answered, squinting against the brightness. 'Don't you know what's going on in Belfast and Derry at all? It's like a different world altogether.'

It was true. These were different worlds from ours. We had seen the pictures on television: the smoke and noise, the surprised faces of the squaddies beneath their helmets, women banging dustbin lids on the pavements as the patrols approached, priests negotiating with RUC officers, soldiers walking backwards between the terraces. It seemed impossible that just two hours on the train could take us from here to there.

'I'd love to get away,' she said.

I can remember watching her as she stretched back

on the grass, with hundreds of tiny freckles smeared across her nose and cheeks. Pinpricks of sweat shone like jewels on her skin and her limbs looked so delicate that they seemed as ready to snap as the hogweed stems around us. A leaf of some plant or other was caught in the buckle of one of her sandals, and the tell-tale bumps of nettle stings clustered around her ankles. When she lay back on the grass, her T-shirt came free from the waistband of her skirt and her bellybutton showed, lengthening as she yawned and stretched some more, the small silver hairs around it glowing in the light. The sun was overhead, the hogweed shadows playing across her chest, which showed the twin bumps of her breasts through her T-shirt. Sometimes she looked as if she had never been born, but had fallen from the stars.

Her mouth, though, came from somewhere else. When I was very young, Ma used to tell me that the fairies had given Catherine her mouth. I knew no different until I started school and the teachers would refer to me as the brother of the girl with the harelip, instinctively touching their own mouths with the tip of a finger. It was a small cleft, a thin white scar that started below her nose and furrowed its way down her lip and into her mouth. I often thought of it as something separate from her, like a mollusc that had taken a hold of her mouth and become so fastened to it that it could never be prised away. Ma had taught her not to be ashamed of her mouth, that it was a gift of difference, and she wore it as a challenge to those who would stop to stare at the beautiful child with the broken mouth.

'What are you gawking at?' she said suddenly, sitting up.

'Nothing.'

I turned aside to look at the sky above us, the tissues of clouds that drifted past, the sun burning a white hole in the blue. When the breeze turned it brought the sounds of the seashore up to us, thick with voices.

I can recall the quality of the sunlight that day as perfectly as if from a photograph held in my hand. The brilliance of it upon Catherine's white T-shirt, the warmth of it spreading across our arms and legs, and the heady smell of diesel rising from the innumerable spills on the ballast below.

Until that summer she had always been a source of wonder for me, like an angel sent from a parallel existence, already free of the awkwardness of childhood, yet still aglow with innocence. On the rare occasions when we were allowed down to the seafront amusements, always at dusk when most of the visitors had disappeared and the molesters had returned to the shadows, Catherine would buy two sticks of candy floss and laugh at me racing from one ride to another. She would watch me soar on the Ferris wheel, an almost solitary figure against an indigo sky, then spin around the dodgem arena with its cracks of electric current and booming music, and pitch tennis balls time and again at worthless china ornaments until the money I had was gone. Afterwards she would take me by the hand and lead me home along the Ways, a narrow passage which wound its way around the backs of the houses, and along which stone had once been brought from the quarry to build the harbour walls. We always walked in silence, our feet echoing on the flagstones, urging me on whenever I paused to wonder at some new Loyalist graffiti the holidaymakers had painted on the walls.

That day, like so many since, did not last. The first sign was a breeze that seemed to travel along the tracks, pushing up against the rhododendrons, which surrendered their light-green underleaves to it. When it reached us I was curled on my side, eyes barely open, Catherine's arm a few inches in front of my face. Her skin burst into goose pimples, the hogweed shadows rocking back and forth across her chest as if an unseen hand were attempting to shake them to nothing. She sat up and gathered her brown cardigan around her.

Mr Wilson was gone from the station platform, a pool of white where one of his ice-cream tubs had fallen over when he went to lift the tray off the flagstones. The tide of voices drifting from the seashore was filling as windbreaks were gathered up and wet swimming costumes peeled from limbs as white as lard, the sudden coolness sending the visitors into the bars, hotels and ice-cream parlours.

4 London

'Sir?'

'Yes?'

'The bell, sir. It's just gone.'

Half of the class are already standing up, pushing and shoving at each other to be first out of the door and into the corridor, where the clamour of the other pupils is rising. I hurriedly scribble their homework exercises on the board as they leave, but only a clutch of the girls can be bothered to wait and write them down.

When they have gone the room is desolate, as if, despite the charts and posters on the walls and the chairs and desks with their ink spills and carvings, no one else has ever set foot in it. It is strange how their absence is always more strongly felt than their presence.

In the staff room there is a discussion about social workers under way. The social workers often visit the school to ask about some of the pupils, whether we have noticed any changes in their behaviour or if they appear more distracted than usual. It is easy to identify those whom we will get asked about, the blankness in their faces, their arms never raised to answer a question, the children whose shoes tap repeatedly against the leg of their desk or who quietly dig the points of pencils into the palms of their hands.

The local authority wants us to treat them differently from the others and Mead, the maths teacher, is arguing against the policy. Some of the other teachers join in and voices are raised, fingers pointed. I stand back near the kettle to watch from a distance. I am too new here to get involved and I can tell from the way the discussion is going that there are other issues and grievances being aired, old rivalries and disagreements dragged out under another guise.

'Michael, isn't it?'

'Aye,' I say, turning from the newspaper which I have spread out on the counter to find the new English teacher standing beside me, spooning instant coffee into a mug. It is her Irish accent that surprises me most, the soft Southern vowels that I have not heard for some time.

'Frances Myers,' she says, offering me her hand. 'I've only just joined.'

'I know – I'm afraid I missed the headmaster's introduction last week. I'm not long here myself.'

'Oh,' she says, filling the mug with boiling water. She holds herself very upright as she pours. The straight angles of her shoulders allow her navy blouse to hang perfectly, her dark bobbed hair just touching the collar. Unlike my own chalk-smeared and sagging corduroys, there is not a single mark or crease on her long navy skirt and her black suede pumps are spotless. There is the hint of a smile on her lips, as if she knows that I am examining her.

'What do you teach?' I ask quickly, although I already know.

'English.'

'Oh, right,'

'And you?'

'Geography.'

'I always liked geography,' she says, smiling.

There is something about her that I can't quite put my finger on; like a buried memory that takes so long to surface that it gets lost along the way.

She has pale, clear skin with the faintest blush of red high on her cheeks and not even a single freckle across her nose. Her eyes are light green, and her eyebrows are as dark and thick as her hair. There is a spareness to her features that is a little unsettling, as though elements have been erased. Everything about her seems measured in some way, from the perfectly fitted clothes to the way she takes small sips of her coffee as she stands there with her ankles crossed, looking across the staff room at the other teachers, who are sitting in a circle, a halo of blue-grey cigarette smoke drifting above their heads.

Suddenly, Mead is on his feet, *The Times* folded in his fist and pointing at Drummond, the history teacher. 'You've changed your tune,' he accuses. Mead's mouth opens and shuts for a while without saying anything before he storms out of the staff room, the closing door sending a draught that scatters the halo of cigarette smoke.

'Somebody isn't happy,' Frances says.

'Not happy at all,' I say, catching her eyes as I turn my attention back from the circle of teachers, which is already breaking up. There is a pause when our eyes meet that seems to go on for an age. I had been about to say something else, but now I can't think what it is.

'Nice to meet you, Michael,' she says, putting her empty mug down on the newspaper and breaking the spell.

'You too,' I say, not looking up as she leaves the staff room.

When she has gone I notice that she has left a lip-stick mark on the edge of the mug, the minute tracings of her flesh like those of a river catchment or delta. With my finger I sweep it into a blur.

Outside, the first traces of drizzle drift aimlessly between the school buildings, speckling the soot-stained red-brick walls. The sky has turned the colour of ash. There are groups of boys in every corner of the yard, sometimes calling out to each other or kicking scuffed leather footballs across the crumbling tarmac.

Beyond the fence and across the canal is a timber yard which once took wood from the barges that brought goods from the Thames and into the heart of the country, a massive shutter door testament to the logs that were swung into the yard on block and tackle. From here I can just see the fresh timbers lying on their racks beneath the corrugated tin roof.

I remember that scent so well. Cut timber in the rain. Birch, ash, willow, pine, cherry, the sap drawn out into the air.

5 Portnew

Da was always busy. Even when work was slack at Easter, Christmas or at the start of the marching season, he would find things to do: a windowsill that needed replacing, a cupboard door to be rehung, a skirting board that had come loose with the passing of years. I would sometimes find him making his way down the stairs, crouching at every step, fingers splayed against the walls to steady himself, listening out for the creak of risers and treads. He would smile and tilt his head to one side to indicate that he was listening, as if for a sign of great importance to us all.

'Do you hear that?' he would say, rocking back and forth on the balls of his feet.

I listened and shook my head. I often heard his own joints cracking and locking as he moved, but there was never any creak in the house that we could hear, the stairs he had rebuilt in the first year of his marriage too true to fail in our lifetimes.

Da had a narrow, lined face which Ma said had been caused by squinting too long at cuts of timber. 'He was handsome when he wooed me,' she was fond of saying. 'If only I'd known!' A cap was perched almost permanently on his head and he would only tip it back when greeting a familiar face or when sizing up a job. He had warm brown eyes that children and women loved, but other men saw as a sign of weakness. He went about his work in a loose chestnut-coloured suit (which a Portstewart tailor had once fitted with extra pockets for the holding of nails, screws and drill bits), a white shirt and a navy tie, his formal appearance surprising new customers when he turned up to give an estimate for a door, a bedstead, a writing desk or a new sash window to replace one that had been eaten away by salt and condensation.

'What is your father up to now?' was my mother's refrain, her hands steeped in the sink, rain falling greyly against the kitchen window. We could hear him above us, tapping away at some part of the structure like a doctor going about with a stethoscope.

'Don't know, Ma,' Catherine and I answered, not lifting our heads from our homework, eager to put in time at the books so that we could be away from the slosh of wet laundry in the sink, the sour smell of boiling meat and bones, the burden of the everyday my mother seemed to wear like a cloak.

'I'm not so sure he knows himself,' came her answer, which was quietly trotted out like the prayers she intoned from hour to hour.

She leaned across the sink to follow the path of a hen that had suddenly bolted from its home, which was an old horsebox in the back yard. She watched it shelter beneath the angle of a downpipe before returning to the safety of its clan, claws scraping for purchase on the slick cobbles.

At the end of the day Da would be released by a knock on the door, Uncle Seamus or another friend asked to stand in out of the rain while a jacket was fetched. 'I'm away out for an hour,' he would call as the door was closed, turning out into the darkening streets, settling the jacket on his shoulders.

On those wet days I noted the imprint of the visitors' soles on the doormat as I went up the stairs to put away my school books: the thick herringbone of a tradesman's shoe, the smooth space of a brogue, the curved groove in the heel of a factory boot.

Catherine would always linger at the table, carefully stacking her brown-paper-clad books on top of each other, watching Ma dragging shirts from the white enamel depths of the sink, the gnarled bar of soap reached for again and again. She watched Ma's nails whitening upon her hands, which were raw-red from water that was close to scalding, steam racing to fog the window and obscure the tremulous hens.

I would listen to them from the bedroom above. Catherine's long and looping questions, always about the family: Ma's uncle, who was looked after by nuns in Armagh, his memory so riddled with holes that he recognized none of us and talked only of his days as an altar boy during the Great War; Uncle Seamus; Aunt Bridie; our cousins in Ardglass; my father's grand-aunt, who lived on an island off Donegal and whom he had not seen since he was Catherine's age. With each retelling Ma would recall some new detail of their lives so that, as she grew older, Catherine committed layer upon layer of family history to memory.

As I played in my room I could hear the murmur of their conversation, rising and falling with the questions and answers. Sometimes words and phrases broke through more clearly than those around them, but out of context they meant nothing to me.

Our street was one of the Terraces, a ladder of streets behind the seafront, built to house the families of men who had worked on the railways. Each house was identical save for the painted doors and window frames. Except ours. Ours had been built in the middle of a terrace and had an arch beside it through which the dray horses that had once dragged the sleepers and rails along the railway would be led to their stables in what would eventually become our back yard. Long after the railway had been completed, the town's milkmen took over the stables, the carts squeezed in together and three small mares occupying the stables. Years later, new rain could still bring the sour dairy smell from between the cobbles.

My grandfather, Da's father, had bought the house from the last of the milkmen and was the first Catholic to live in the Terraces, ignoring the paint that had been thrown at the house during the first few years, the stinking rubbish tipped at the doorstep, the window glass scraped with coins. In time more Catholics moved into the Terraces and the trouble died down, but some neighbours still passed each other in the street without exchanging a word.

Da would always return from the pub in time to carve the joint of ham or pork my mother lifted steaming from the aluminium pot when she heard the front door pushed open. The scour of the carving knife against the sharpening steel was our call to the table, the feet of the wooden chairs squeaking on the steam-slicked tiled floor as we dragged them out to sit. Ma was always last to the table, shuttling back and forth from the cooker with bowls of vegetables. Da would ask her to sit so that he could say a prayer, but she would insist on standing, knotting her hands in her apron, the words slipping by her lips, sitting only when all was done and the meal half eaten.

'It's wasted on you now,' Da protested as she

unravelled the apron strings and let them fall about the chair. He pointed at the meat on her plate. 'The heat is gone out of it, don't you know that?'

She knew, but she would always be last to the table.

It was different when Uncle Seamus stayed on for the evening meal. Uncle Seamus was Ma's younger brother and he helped Da out whenever he could, which was often. He didn't have Da's instinct with wood but he was good with numbers, and whenever possible Da would get Seamus to measure a job and order the wood from Elson's timber yard. Never more than a few inches of wood would be left over, even on the biggest jobs. He was fast at laying joists, the gaps always perfectly judged so that the boards could bend enough for comfort but were stiff enough for strength. He always made sure to ask what floorboards would be going down so that he could lay the joists accordingly, adjusting for pine, ash, beech or whatever. He could put up shelves, hang a door and frame a window, but the finer work was not his and he knew it, happy to watch Da making up a gramophone cabinet, a card table or a chest of drawers and not want the same craft for himself.

When Da and Seamus came in from a job or the workshop they would sit in the front room and open bottles of Guinness, which they drank in silence, Da leaning far back in the armchair, Seamus sitting forward on the couch, the bottle held in both hands, his elbows perched on his knees. The room filled with the sweet freshness of wood from their clothes and the curdled smell of the bottled stout. Catherine and I would slide into the room and stand at the window to watch them, the light draining through the sheer nets at the window. Da was silent and it was always Seamus who broke.

'H-how are ye getting along at s-school?' Even in summer that topic was constant: counting the weeks before school would start again, enquiring about the books that needed to be bought and covered to allow them to survive the passage through Catherine's year to mine.

'Fair enough,' came our inevitable answer.

Catherine would announce that she had scored high in maths or history or science, and Seamus would ask her the simplest questions to prove her skills. 'What year was the s-siege of Derry?' 'Divide one hundred and f-forty-four by eleven?' 'What's the s-scientific symbol for lead?'

Seamus clapped when she answered, and she smiled as though the weak light from the window fell for her alone. I stood in the shadows, watching her perform.

We always asked for the jokes he told in the workshop, the ones that caused Da to smile and straighten from the bench to wonder at the easy humour, the way Seamus would break from the telling with his own laughing as the punchline came to mind. But the jokes,

Seamus explained, were not to be heard in the house at
all, and he'd keep them for when we were older. Da
muttered his agreement, swiping froth from his lip with
the tip of his tongue.

Ma called us to the table, the bottles of stout carried
in to be finished with the meal. Seamus was always
careful to wait for Ma to sit before he would start.

'Go on, you,' Da encouraged him. 'You could be
waiting for ever and the good food wasted.'

'Aye.'

Seamus would pick up his knife and fork, but
nothing would be eaten until she was sitting opposite
him.

And always towards the end of the meal that was
taken at the same time every day came the peal of bells
from the Protestant chapel on the other side of the
Ways. The chapel stood between our house and the
railway station, and although we tried our best to
ignore the bells, we could not. With the start of the
violence in the cities they seemed to peal louder and
longer. Da sometimes laid his cutlery down and gripped
the edge of the table, knuckles whitening with the anger
that buckled within him. Ma ate and Seamus bowed
his head.

There was real silence then as we waited for the last
bell to fade, the blood returning to Da's hands, the
ticking of cutlery on plates coming through the tension
that only slowly leaked away.

6 London

Frances Myers moves about the school like an angel, her skin aglow, undimmed by the dusty gloom of the classrooms and corridors. Through the glass panel in her classroom door I see her standing with a textbook perfectly balanced in the palm of her hand, or sitting upright at the desk, her soft clear vowels travelling around the room and commanding the full attention of each and every one of her pupils. The blackboard is filled with her copperplate handwriting, the words so perfectly formed in chalk that it looks as if she has spent the whole morning writing them out. When she sees me at the window she winks as she turns away from her class, the slightest of smiles upon her lips.

'Are you coming for a drink this evening?' I ask her one Friday.

She hesitates and gazes down into her cup of coffee.

'A few of us sometimes go to the Island Queen a

little bit down the way for a drink or two,' I add, afraid that she thinks it would be just the two of us.

'I know where it is,' she says. 'Let me know when you're going.' She smiles and turns to look at the newspaper spread out on the counter, her shoe tapping against the floor tiles.

After the last bell I wait outside her classroom, the children squeezing through the door and making for the common room, where their coats hang on hooks.

When she comes out I notice that a diamanté cross has snagged on one of the buttons of her blouse and point it out to her.

'Thanks,' she says, pinching the cross between her lips and untwining the silver chain. She lets the cross drop down between her breasts and I find myself wondering what her skin feels like there. When I look up she is smiling.

'I'm quite keen to get home, Michael,' she says when I ask if she's coming to the pub. 'It's been a long week. You know how it is.'

'Aye,' I say, but my heart is sinking. 'Good night, then.'

'Good night, Michael. See you next week.'

'Aye.'

The Island Queen is full of its usual Friday afternoon crowd. Everyone seems exhausted at the end of the week, as if the effort of going home from here is too much for them and they would prefer to stay in this languid cocoon with its blue smoke atmosphere and nicotine-stained walls.

'Who's in the chair?' Mead says, turning to face the rest of us as we sit down around the table beside the jukebox.

'You are,' someone points out sharply.

'So I am, so I am,' Mead says, fumbling about in his pockets for his wallet.

I only stay for the first drink, my attention wandering to the street that is beyond the etched windows. I think of Frances walking home, the way she carries herself as if wearing a suit of armour. I barely hear their goodbyes as I leave.

Ten minutes later I find her dawdling at the window of one of the many antique shops in Camden Passage, her hands sunk in her pockets, stooping a little to peer at a locket or bracelet set upon the crushed black velvet of a display case. When I come up behind her, it is my reflection in the glass that she sees first.

'Hello, Michael,' she says without turning around.

'I only stayed for the one,' I explain.

She taps at the window. 'Isn't it beautiful?' She points to a silver brooch in the shape of a rising sun.

'Art deco?' I offer.

'Late Victorian,' she says.

'You seem to know what you're talking about.'

'You don't, that's for sure.'

When I look at her face in the window I see that she

is smiling, the smoothness of her features interrupted now by soft lines and creases.

'My mother used to collect Victoriana,' she says. 'I'd know it anywhere, but I wouldn't have a clue about the rest.' She straightens up and flicks her hair back over the edge of her collar with her fingers.

'Your mother died, is that it?' I venture.

'No, she's alive, but she stopped collecting it after my father died. She said it made her think of the mornings she used to drag him up and down the Francis Street shops. It made her feel bad because he was never interested. He only went because she wanted him to.'

'I'm sorry.'

'There's no need to be. It was a long time ago.'

On the way up the street, beneath the tall plane trees of the Green, which are just coming into leaf, she tells me about how little she knows of the city, how the size of it is completely bewildering to her and how she has only recently moved here from Dublin. She had spent a few months the previous summer on a curriculum course in Leeds, but nothing prepared her for London.

'In at the deep end,' I say, and we both smile.

'Anything for a fresh start,' she sighs, lifting the strap of her satchel onto her shoulder.

'A fresh start after what?' I say, but her face is turned away.

All around us the office and shop workers are making their way to the many bars that line the High

Street we are leaving behind, unbuttoning jackets and loosening ties as they dash across the black and white panels of the zebra crossings. Buses empty more and more of them onto the pavements, swinging from the pole on the platform, anxious to secure their seats for the evening.

I remember the Derry bus that stopped in Portnew, the coughing diesel engine that would wake the town as it waited on the assembly workers who hurried up the hill, half-eaten slices of toast gripped between their teeth. The heater was usually broken and on winter mornings the workers would pull their knees up beneath their chins and hide their heads behind their collars to keep the cold at bay, closing their eyes in the vain hope of a few minutes' extra sleep.

'Where do you live?' Frances asks as another bus shudders past.

'Just a few minutes away, on Northbank Avenue, near the petrol station. Do you know it?'

She shakes her head.

'And you?'

There is the slightest of checks in her stride and I know that she is wondering whether she should tell me. 'In Stoke Newington,' she says hesitantly, 'off the High Street. I've a little flat above a Jewish family.'

'Do you like it there?'

'I haven't made up my mind about the place yet. It's

very noisy at night, although the Jewish family don't make a sound.'

'I suppose you can always move if you find you don't like the place.'

'It won't be as easy as that, I'm afraid,' she says. 'My mother insisted I buy somewhere to live – she gave me the money for the deposit and I have an uncle in Bristol who secured the mortgage. I'm stuck there whether I like it or not.'

'It's no harm having an asset like that under your belt.'

'My mother and father moved around a lot after they were first married because he couldn't settle anywhere. She hated it and she's so terrified I'll take after him that she insisted I buy the flat. It's a point of principle with her – she wasn't even bothered having a look at it.'

I tell her about the flat I rent with two others, a telephone salesman and another teacher. The house is dilapidated but the rent is cheap. An Italian family live in the basement flat and their shouting and arguing carry through the whole house. We often stop to listen to an argument, a crescendo of cursing before a door is slammed, shaking the house, footsteps at the front gate, which is slammed too. She laughs when I tell her that because one of the bedrooms in the flat is no bigger than a cupboard, we move rooms every three months to make it fair.

'No one could live too long in that wee room without going a bit soft in the head,' I counter. 'There's more space in a prison cell.'

We walk on along the darkening street, gutters that are filled with the blackened sheddings of cherry blossom, traces of pink along their edges like lipstick marks on paper.

Ahead of us is the neon sign of the petrol station where I must turn off towards home. I do not want this hour to end.

'This must be you,' she says when we reach the petrol station.

'I'll walk you home,' I say. 'It's getting dark.'

'There's no need for that, Michael,' she says. 'I know my way and there's plenty of people about.' She straightens an imaginary crease from her coat. Her face looks even paler now under the sodium glow of the streetlights that have been coming on while we walk, following us up the street. In its strange way the light makes her more beautiful, gives more expression to her face, defines the shallow ridge of her cheekbones, the line of her nose. It throws shadows from above that make something about her look wrong, out of pro-portion or lacking symmetry – I cannot tell.

When I protest she smiles and says no again. She pulls the collar of her coat up about her face as if to close me out.

'Well, I'll see you on Monday, then,' I say.

'Of course. I'm there *every* Monday.' She smiles before turning off up the road, headlights tracking her steps. Her hands are sunk in her pockets and her shoulders are pulled tight.

For a moment I want to run after her and put my arm around those stiff shoulders, but I know that that would destroy everything.

7 Portnew

Summer came to an early and sudden end in Portnew the year of the moon landings. We spent that July with the radio always on and turned up loud so that the latest news from Cape Canaveral would not be missed. We crowded into Glennon's front room, the only one of our Catholic neighbours with a television. Our Das and Mas told us to hush as the screen filled first with pictures of crowds in Derry holding placards in their hands and marching through the streets, RUC men and B Specials standing behind rows of Land Rovers with their batons drawn, priests and politicians appealing for calm. Impatiently we watched Bernadette Devlin being interviewed time and again until eventually we cheered as the astronauts came on the screen and we settled to marvel at the sight of the rocket waiting on the launch pad, count the days to take-off and examine every detail of the crude drawings that

illustrated the path the rocket would take towards the
moon.

Day after day, bands of rain washed in upon the
tide, darkening the sand and raising a sour smell from
the foreshore. The amusement arcades smeared the far
end of the seafront with a sickly light in the late afternoons, hoping to tempt groups of bored children with
pocket money to spend. They crowded around the one-
armed bandits to watch the coins being fed, the arms
being pulled, the dials ringing, jabbing at the displays
with their fingers, drifting away empty-handed.

On days like these I would go to watch Da in his
workshop at the back of the house. Da worked beneath
two great ship's lanterns that hung on chains from the
cross-beams and filled the room with a strong yellow
glow.

A huge deal workbench dominated the workshop,
vice grips bolted along its edges, a circular-saw blade
emerging from its middle like the keel of a yacht.
Ranged out on the bench were a dozen chisels, their
handles striped black and yellow like wasps, blades
newly smeared with oil and already collecting the
sawdust that forever hung in the air. In a corner of
the workshop stood another bench upon which a lathe
was fixed. The maker's logo, Coronet Tool Company,
had been almost rubbed away by the action of Da's
hand. In wonder I had often watched Da haul the lathe

into the kitchen to strip it down, the gleaming mechanism laid out on the tiles.

At the far end of the workshop, where very little light ever shone, was the loft. In the days when the workshop had been a stable, bags of feed and bales of hay for the horses had been stored there, away from mice and the damp that had slicked the cobbles. Now only wood was stored there and the drop ladder had been removed, Da and Uncle Seamus hopping up onto the big bench to push the long timbers into place. I was never allowed up there and could only imagine the view of the workshop and the giddy drop down to the bench and cobbles below, the thick darkness that seemed to sleep there upon the timbers like a living thing.

'Go on now and switch on the lathe for me,' Da said, moving along the length of the two-by-two with a steel rule, licking the point of a pencil before tracing lines across the wood, his face bent close to the grain like a watchmaker.

I had to stand on a stool to reach the socket for the lathe. The suddenness of the loud hum it made always startled me and I had to spread my arms to steady myself on the stool.

I watched Da putting on the big protective glasses, lifting his cap to fit the elastic around the back of his head, his eyes looming fish-like behind the thick plastic lens. When Da set to work with the lathe, curled pieces of wood would suddenly spring into the air, tapping off the thick glasses and catching in his clothes.

I sat up on the workbench and watched him move through the different chisels, less and less wood coming away with each smaller blade until he was down to a chisel little bigger than a nail, cutting channels into a baluster. Every so often he would take a chisel and lift the glasses to examine its blade, sometimes sharpening it on the new Arkansas oilstone beside him.

With each baluster that was completed the floor at Da's feet filled with spiral shavings, thin filigrees of wood that were almost as soft as new wool. Afterwards I would collect them into plastic bags, and on Saturday mornings they would be sold for pocket money to the man who ran a pet shop behind the garage in Market Street.

With dusk the poor light from outside thinned away to nothing and the shadows in the far end of the workshop deepened. Sometimes I imagined the ghosts of the dray horses shifting in their darkened stalls, my imagination fuelled by the sound of mice making their way through the cut-offs collected beneath the hayloft. Whenever I stood in that space beneath the loft I would close my eyes and try to summon the ammonia and milk smell that would once have hung so heavily there.

It was dark when Uncle Seamus appeared at the door.

'Good man yourself, Shamie!' Da exclaimed. 'Just the man I need to rub these balusters down.'

'You've made n-nice work out of them, that's for s-sure,' Seamus said, lifting one of the posts up and squinting against the strong lights so that he could examine its profile. 'There's little enough r-rubbing needed on them. S-Sure, even the young fella could do it.' He brought the post over to me, the solid weight of it in his hand, balanced like a good hammer.

I hardly noticed Uncle Seamus's stammer, but those who knew him less well were often disarmed or amused by it, the way his jaw would hang open and empty while the missing syllable travelled so slowly up from his throat. I watched them trying not to smile, their foreheads creasing with the effort, sometimes mouthing the word to themselves or saying it out loud. He hated when others attempted to fill in the gaps for him, a sinking look upon his face, the rest of the sentence trailing away to nothing.

Uncle Seamus had small blue eyes that darted about as he spoke, never holding your own for a moment and only steadying with the effort of freeing the syllables that stuck. Even though he was still young his ginger hair had begun to thin at the crown so that his scalp was already heavily freckled, and together with his beard this made him look much older than his years. Da used to ask some of the regulars in Cassidy's, the bar they both favoured after a day's work, if they would lay a bet with him that they could put an age upon Seamus that was accurate to within two years. The men would take one look at Seamus and decline the offer, laughing for a while before asking what age he really was. But Da and Seamus never said, and I never found out either.

Uncle Seamus looked at me and grinned. 'Would you rub the p-posts down for your Da, w-would you?'

'Aye,' I said, leaping down from where I had been sitting on the bench, giddy at the chance to help the men out.

Da put his hand on my head and laughed. 'Stay where you are now, son. Your uncle will smooth them down this time. It wouldn't do for them to be rubbed against the grain if your hand was to slip. Another time.'

It was always another time, the chance to help out and work with the older men lost again to Da's fear that the slightest flaw might destroy his reputation. A slip like that would be noticed by no one but himself.

While they smoothed the balusters I swept up the shavings and dumped them into a plastic bag beside the door. A red and silver horseshoe magnet hung on a long piece of baling twine and I took it down to sweep it through the shavings in the bag. Stray nails, pins and tacks could be recovered in this way so that the pet shop owner could not complain that an animal had been injured or a child's thumb pricked.

Behind me I could hear Uncle Seamus telling Da about the news that the British Army would be sending troops to Derry and Belfast to help the RUC cope with the trouble that the civil rights marchers had started.

Something seemed to move in the loft above me and I thought again of the ghosts of the dray horses shifting in their stalls. I shivered and went back to where Da and Seamus were smoothing the balusters, the minute smoothings drifting to the floor like chalk dust.

'They're m-marching because they can't get the w-work and homes they want, Jack,' Seamus was saying, reaching across the workbench to emphasize his point, the strong yellow light catching in the curls of his red hair. 'If you lived in the cities, Jack, you'd know what it was like not to get w-work just because you went to M-Mass of a Sunday morning.'

Seamus took hold of the baluster Da was inspecting. 'There's m-men like you and me, Jack,' he said when Da looked up, 'put out of their homes as well as their j-jobs. Wives and weans just thrown out with them. No homes, Jack, no w-work to be had, and no one to s-stop it.' Seamus let go of the baluster. 'It's not r-right, not r-right at all,' he finished.

While I cleared the pieces of metal from the magnet Da and Seamus's voices rose higher and higher. I never liked to hear people argue, and it was rare to hear Da and Seamus getting angry about something.

'And will the troops give them work and homes, is that it?' Da was saying.

'Ah, you're being s-stupid now.' Seamus went to the door and looked out for a moment, his foot scratching in the sawdust like one of the hens in the yard. 'There's some saying that the RA will have to do something about it or every Catholic will be run out of their home by Christmas.'

'There's too much talk of the RA these days.' Da rose.

'But it m-might put the fear of G-God into the Prot-estants and stop the trouble once and for all.'

Da pushed his cap back on his forehead and sighed, the baluster laid down on the workbench with a sharp knock. No matter how hard Seamus tried to engage him in argument about the marches and the soldiers, he would not respond, his lips thinning with determin-ation until Seamus gave up.

'Go on into the house there like a good man, Seamus,' Da said when he could bear the tension no longer.

'Aye, I might as well. I'm getting nowhere here.'

Da smiled at me when Seamus had left. 'Take no heed of your uncle, son, take no heed.'

'OK, Da,' I said, tying the last bag closed.

'The thing is,' Da began, 'he has a point, but I'll not let him have the pleasure of winning it.'

I nodded, but I didn't know what Da meant.

When the tools had been put away and the lathe switched off and covered with the oilcloth, Da lifted me up onto the wooden bench as he often did before giving me a shilling for helping him with the tidying.

'Michael,' he sighed, 'wee Michael.' He drew his book of names from the pocket of his jacket. Da recorded the details of every customer, who they were related or connected to and what their business was, between the leatherette covers of that notebook. Now, as he flicked it open, the edge seemed more frayed than ever before. Stiff with ink, the pages made a crackling noise like something aflame. 'Do you mind the people who won't have me do work for them any more, son?'

I hesitated, trying to put names to the faces I remembered: Cartin, Warren, Fellowes, Wilson, Tarrant, Robinson. 'Aye,' I said.

'It pains me to see them written here,' he began, glancing at the pages of the notebook. 'I can't stop thinking of the good work I did for them over the years. The best of timber and sweat and elbow grease went into some of that work and they might as well tear it down now for all I care.'

He took out his fountain pen, uncapped it and flicked a bead of ink from the nib. Flattening the pages of the notebook, he began to read through the names.

'Phillips?'

'No, Da.'

'Bingham?

'No, Da.'

'Curtin, Desmond Curtin.'

'No, Da.'

'Curtin has a cousin married to a Catholic off in Kilkeel,' Da said. 'They run a guesthouse in the town there. They might need work doing at some time.'

'It's a long way away, Da.'

'I suppose it is, and Curtin wouldn't put in a word for me now on any account.'

I watched him draw the pen across Curtin's name and then Bingham's, a picture of Bingham's shop front coming to me, black suspenders strapped across plastic hips, the small hooks of brassieres, the blank-faced mannequins, yellow and orange cards advertising the range of sizes available inside, the tiny bell suspended on a tin spring beyond the door.

'Harding?'

'No, Da.'

'Aye.'

The pen drawn across this name as others before and countless more afterwards, the town splitting in two, the links that could now be made between all those who had been struck out, like the faces in the small frames Ma moved from the mantelpiece to the sideboard as they passed on.

Da slipped the notebook back into his jacket and fumbled around in his trouser pockets. He always did this when he was about to give me a coin, pretending that he had nothing to give me. Finally he came up with a shilling sitting in his opened palm.

'For me, Da?' I said.

'Aye, for you. You're a good lad.' Da bent over and put his hands on my temples and kissed me on the forehead. 'You're a good lad,' he said again.

When I heard another noise in the loft I looked up, expecting to see a mouse skimming across a joist, its tiny limbs busy like clock workings. Instead, Catherine peered out of the gloom, her face as white as the sawn ends of the boards upon which she had flattened herself out of sight. I almost cried out with surprise, but when Catherine raised a finger to her lips I managed to stop myself and started coughing, as if a bubble of air was trapped in my throat.

'Are you all right, son?' Da asked. 'Come away from there now. There must be an inch of dust under that loft.'

When I looked up again Catherine had flattened herself against the boards and only the inky sheen of her hair could be seen. While Da was putting away the pan and brush and getting ready to close up for the night, I peered into the loft, where Catherine lay still upon the boards, breathing the dark air where the hay bales and barley sacks were once stored, and where only ghosts should be.

*

It was not long after that evening that the letters appeared on our alley wall. IRA. Spelled out in white paint that leaked into the red bricks of the gap through which we passed into the back yard. There were trails of the paint on the cobbles where it had run from their brushes, the edge of a careless footprint which I could not identify as factory boot, hobnail or plimsoll.

Ma saw it first when she went to hang clothes on the line in the yard, the letters gleaming in the gloom. She called Da out from his breakfast and I went after him to see what it was about. He touched the paint and his finger came away with a patch of white on its tip. Ma watched him, the bundle of damp clothes still gathered between her arms, her eyes wetting with tears.

Da laid his hand on her wrist as he came past. 'Never you mind. It's nothing to worry about.'

'Inside!' he said firmly, and I retreated to the back door.

He came back from the workshop with a blue tin of Jeyes Fluid and poured the best part of it into a bucket. As I listened to the water drumming from the outside tap into the galvanized bottom of the bucket, I watched Ma hanging up the washing, the shaking that had started in her causing some of the wooden clothes-pegs to fall to the ground.

When Catherine came down she announced that 'IRA' had been painted on the walls of the railway station earlier in the week. 'And someone's painted

"Fuck the Pope" out at the end of the old pier,' she added. 'Right beside where the life-ring used to be. Do you mind it?'

I nodded. There was graffiti going up everywhere, on lampposts, doors, walls, trees, on anything that could be marked, as if the words and slogans had always been there and were only now emerging from beneath the layers of paint, stone and bark.

When I went out to Da later the letters were still visible, the paint clinging to the texture of the bricks, lying thickly in the pointing. Da said he'd get rid of the last of them later. But the letters never came away and within a week they were back to their prime, the paint applied thicker than before and earlier in the night so that by dawn it was dry and secure. In his anger Da threw the bucket along with the water at the letters, the handle buckling as it clattered off the wall, along the cobbles and out into the street, bringing Mrs Doody to her window across the way. Da smiled at her as he retrieved the bucket, the twist in the handle reminding us all of those days each time we filled it from the tap.

One morning, as we left for school, Catherine steered me towards the Union Jack flags which had been painted on the gables of Simmons Street, the closest Protestant street to ours.

My heart began to thump the closer we got to the

enormous flags, and I watched the rows of identical doors for signs of the youths who lived there.

We stood beneath one of the flags. The paint had already begun to leach into the red brick so that deltas of red and blue and white made their way down the gable.

'Look!' Catherine whispered, grabbing my shoulder.

The kerbstones on Simmons Street had all been painted in red and blue and white, and there were dozens of footprints on the pavements where children had walked through the fresh paint.

A door opened nearby and a group of young boys spilled out, shrugging into coats and jackets, the smooth dome of a head inside a jumper that was being stretched on. We quickly turned back the way we had come, scuttling across Donald Lane toward the safety of our own street.

'Taigs! Papist cowards!' The taunts followed us along the house fronts, and every part of me bristled in anticipation of the stones that might come but did not.

'Leave them alone, will you, they're only weans,' came a mother's voice, calling them away to school.

Still the clamour of their taunts hung in the air and we did not stop running until we were past every house in our street and turning onto Welwyn Road.

Catherine was laughing between deep breaths,

leaning against a windowsill, her hands pinched at her waist where she was complaining of a stitch.

'That was a great laugh, wasn't it, Michael?' she said.

I looked at her. 'What do you mean?'

'Having a dig at the Prods.'

'I suppose so,' I said, my breath struggling back with a sawing sound. 'Will they come looking for us, do you think?'

'Don't be stupid. They couldn't be bothered.'

For days afterwards I kept tight to the houses and the walls for fear of being seen by any of the crowd who had chased us away, slowing at blind corners, dashing across streets once I was sure there was no one about. In truth I would not have recognized the boys if I had walked straight into them, but that simple, barely founded fear marked a change in the character and the geography of the town for me; streets, factories and shops echoing now with more than the clatter and clamour of play and trade, newly resonant with a badness borne in the blood.

8 London

The smell of the canal, of something long-decayed yet returning to life, drifts through the window and steals about the classroom. The smell was worse in April, when the first strong sun rose above the redundant warehouses and the timber yard to strike the sleeping waters, but the windows had been closed against the squalls of showers that scratched the glass then suddenly poured over it in streams before falling away to leave fingers of rain clawing the panes.

I found Frances at the schoolyard fence a few days after I had left her in the street, her fingers curled through the rusting wire, shivering slightly in the cold. A supermarket trolley gleamed dully in the canal water below us. When I asked her if she had made it home safely the other night, she said that she was sorry to have refused my offer, but she didn't want people to think that she couldn't look out for herself.

'I know,' I said. 'There's nothing wrong with that. Don't apologize.'

'I just felt bad about it afterwards, that's all.'

'Aye, but that was no skin off my nose.'

'You could walk me home another time,' she said, unstitching her fingers from the wire and turning to me.

I looked away. The signs were rotting on the timber yard, grey-green algae that crept up from the canal. Soon they would slide into its still waters.

'Michael?'

'Aye,' I said. 'That would be nice.'

She smiles when we meet later at the top of the stairs, her arms filled with folders.

'Can I help you with that wee bundle there?'

'No thanks, Michael. I'm just going to dump them in the staff room.'

A group of children pushes past us, knocking one of the folders onto the stairs.

'Slow down or you'll kill yourselves on the stairs!' I shout after them, handing the folder to Frances.

'So what?' one of them calls back.

Frances leaves the folders on the long trestle table beneath the window in the staff room that is thick with plastic coffee cups and discarded photocopies and pages that have come away from other folders, their corners turned inwards by the sun like shed leaves, the grey husks of bluebottles and the faded stripes of last season's wasps scattered among them.

'I'm off to a film tonight,' Frances says when we step outside.

'Good for you. What'll you see?'

'I don't know. Maybe the new Woody Allen film. We'll decide when we get to the West End. It's something to do in the middle of the week – it breaks the days up.'

She is wearing fresh perfume, a rich scent, like something drawn from the centre of an orchid. In this bright light her eyes look somewhere between pale green and blue. Her skin glows.

'Who are you going with?' I ask.

Her face goes distant in a smile. I should not have asked, but I want it to be me who sits beside her in the bristling dark of the cinema, listening to her breathe in the silence between scenes, that orchid smell lingering.

'Nobody you would know,' is all she says eventually.

As we walk to the underground station we say nothing except when we enter the narrow park at Colebrooke Row where the flower beds have been newly planted and are ablaze with wallflowers and tulips like a fire taken to the black earth, the colours flickering in the shadows of cherry blossom and plane trees.

'My grandfather would have been proud of a display like that,' Frances remarks. 'He was a great one for bedding plants. People used to gather at his front gate to gawk at the display and some even took photographs. He hated their praise but I still remember him standing invisibly behind the net curtains in his front room, smiling with pleasure at the attentions of the passers-by.'

'Where are you going, then?' she asks while we wait for the train on the impossibly narrow platform.

I had followed her without thinking, walking to the station for the sake of company and the chance to simply be with her. 'To the South Bank,' I manage. 'There's music in the foyer tonight.'

'That's nice,' she says.

'It's something to do.'

People gather on the platform while we wait, all the time shuffling closer to the white line, some looking for a familiar advertising poster which tells them where to stand when the doors open. A pair of mice chase each other around the black space beneath the rails that I have heard called the suicide pit, their furred tails sometimes brushing against the third live rail. The train draws in and we stand aside to let the passengers out, but once the doorways have cleared there come those few seconds when none of us wants to be the first into the train. Frances makes the break and the rest of us follow her into the carriage.

Frances rests her satchel across her knees and draws her heels in tight against the row of seats in the manner that most Londoners adopt so that they cannot be accused of taking up too much space. For someone so new to the city she is learning fast.

I watch her reflection in the window opposite, her eyes tracking the advertisements above the passengers' heads, the edge of her thumb idly turning a thread that has come loose from the strap of her satchel. Her features shift and turn unsteadily in the glass as the carriage shudders and rocks, assembling and reassembling. Sometimes there are two of her in the glass, like the changes I find in her: open one moment and distant the next, as if she fears that in sharing something of herself with me she will lose it for ever.

When the train begins to slow she stands up. 'I change here,' she says. She lifts her hand to the side of her face and gives me a little wave as she steps off.

'See you tomorrow,' I say, and she smiles.

As the train pulls into the tunnel again I look for her among the multitude on the platform. She is being squeezed on all sides by people making for the stairs and escalators. Her hair spills out from behind her ears and down across her forehead. She leaves it be. She seems lost in herself until at the last moment she looks up and sees me turning in my seat, the palm of my hand pressed against the glass. Her eyes widen and words come to her lips but the tunnel closes them out before I can know what they are.

*

Rudderless I change at Euston, drifting along the passageways and escalators until I find the ticket hall with its rows of queues, the scrape of bags and briefcases being pushed along the floor. A few charity workers move about the queues, shaking donation boxes at the passengers, who seem to want to make out that they are blind.

REPENT! REPENT! The harsh rattle of the coins is the same cry as that of the Protestant zealots who stood outside the railway station in Portnew, their hands fluttering with fragments of scripture printed on cheap paper, collection boxes hung about their necks with string. They stood in their black among the other hawkers: Mr Wilson, the barber, who sold ice cream when business was slow on the rare hot days, a tray of vanilla and strawberry cups hanging from his neck, the smooth imprint of a scissors handle on the knuckle of his thumb; a woman sold sticks of rock from a pram, the red seam of letters from another seaside town altogether, the plastic wrappers gone stiff and crackling to splinters even as she handed them out to the visiting Belfast children who bought them. In idle moments Catherine and I would taunt her with her fraud and she would rush the pram at us, the old springs squealing like an animal woken from slumber, the scratch of stones in our sandals as we fled, Catherine's laugh.

I return to the Northern Line platform, drawn by its familiar smell of distantly burning newspaper. The platform is completely empty and when a train finally arrives nobody gets off, the guard leaning from his post to signal to the driver before the doors rattle shut behind me.

The girl is framed in the window of the door to the next carriage when I notice her for the first time. My mouth dries up and something begins to coil inside my chest. Everything in the train begins to seem impossibly loud and clear, the scrape of wheels on metal track, the hush of hydraulics, the soughing breath of the passengers. As the train curves into bends she disappears from view before reappearing again, hair brushed to one side of her face, her nose shallow and hardly flared, eyebrows arched as if in intense interest at everything around her. Her skin is as pale as the insides of eggshells. Her hand is folded across her mouth so that I cannot see her lips. Sometimes she sweeps her hair back behind her ears, but still that mouth is never seen.

As the train slows into each station my heart rises in my chest. I am afraid that she will get up and leave but she stays in her seat, her body shuddering a little as the train takes off. When someone comes to stand between me and the window I move to the next seat so that I can keep my eyes on her.

A man's briefcase bumps into her knees as he passes and she says something in answer to his apology. I think I hear the faint Ulster ring of her voice, the drawn vowels that have been softened by the dozen and more years since I last heard her speak.

I cannot believe it is her. I cannot see her mouth, and yet she holds herself the same way, with that bored detachment from the world, those eyes that seem blank but are taking everything in. She seems hardly to have changed, except that the hand to the mouth is new, as if she has become ashamed of her difference. There are no creases that I can see upon her skin, and her fingers are like those of a young girl. Those years, those times, cannot have aged her so little.

The train screeches around another bend and when the carriages straighten again her seat is empty. I push my way towards the window and see that the doorways of her carriage are filled with people waiting to get off, anxiously edging about on the tread boards as the slowing of the train pushes their bodies together. From the crowd emerges a pale and narrow wrist reaching for an overhead rail, the fingers searching for grip.

Out on the platform it seems that I have lost her, the crowds making for the stairs too thick to push through. Then people part just enough for me to catch the back of her head among the dozens in front. Seconds later I lose sight of her before she reappears at the foot of the stairs.

'Catherine!' When I call out to her my voice is reedy with panic so that I hardly recognize it. 'Catherine!' I call again, but she does not change, the frame of her shoulders shifting from side to side as she goes up the stairs, her eyes, like everyone else's, on the metal-edged steps at her feet.

I race up the escalator, my elbows knocking into other passengers. Someone shouts at me after I stumble against them but I don't even check my stride. I know that if I can get to the top in time I can watch her ascent. I examine the faces as they come up, row after row of them on the bank of escalators emerging like dazzled moles. I wait until the multitude has thinned to a few. She is not among them. I make my way back down to the platforms but she is not there either.

When I reach the Embankment the lines of bulbs that link the lamp standards are rocking gently on the breeze that travels the river. Illuminated train carriages flicker like movie reel through the iron mesh of Hungerford Bridge. Everything goes still, the hours drawing slowly to a halt.

The face of the girl on the train returns to me and I match it to what I remember of Catherine. If it *was* her, she is as lost to me now as she has ever been, swallowed up by the streets, the buildings, the people, returned to her other life.

9 Portnew

Ma was always first to hear the Lambeg drums. She put it down to the hens in the back yard, ears alert to every new sound that might suggest a threat. She watched them from her station at the sink, where she usually stood, washing, ironing, chopping meat or vegetables on the piece of beech that Da had cut to fit around the taps so that she could work with a view of the back yard no matter what she was doing. Even when she stopped working to take a cup of tea, she would insist on standing at that sink, the cup between her hands, gazing out at the worn cobbles, the workshop, the hen-house, the laundry decked out on the line, the black roofs of the houses on the street that backed onto ours. It was no view at all, but it seemed enough for her.

The drums began in June, and I always associated their sound with the last weeks of school before the summer break; classes sometimes taken in the shade of the horse chestnut tree beside the gate, the sun slanting into the classroom so that the chalk on the board faded in the glare and we had to leave our seats and crowd around it to copy down what had to be learned overnight. The sound of the drums sailed in through the open windows, twisting on the breeze so that it seemed nearby one moment and distant the next.

The men from the Orange Lodge spent most of the long June evenings practising in the Orange Hall, the muffled boom of Mr Bingham's Lambeg accompanied by the drone of the crumbling tin roof. The fifes arrived later, Mr Cooke and his three sons coming through the thin twilight which danced on the chrome fittings of their instrument cases. The mock leather was blackened with shoe polish for the season and the instruments smelled of the tarnish remover which blistered their lips on the first practice.

We listened to them from the other side of the padlocked fire door, sitting amidst shadows where we couldn't be seen, Catherine drawing her knees up under her skirt so that the whiteness of bare skin would not mark us out. Midges filled the air around us, rising and falling on unseen currents, scattering whenever we batted them away, only to regroup within seconds. We compared bites, taking pride in a half-dozen on the back of a knuckle or the milky reverse of a wrist. We were more wary of the wasps and horse flies that visited the empty beer bottles and lemonade bottles stacked in plastic crates beside the door, Catherine pushing me over as she rushed to escape their attentions.

Their playing was uncertain during the first sessions. There were movements that had to be relearned and notes that had to be refound. Catherine nudged me whenever one of the Cooke boys fell out of tune, the notes going further and further away from the rest of the playing until it became irretrievable and he was forced to stop, Bingham's frustration spilling over into anger.

'A fine sound that'll be on the Twelfth, boy. A fine sound. The Taigs'll be laughing at us, they will, laughing. Doubled over, boy.'

They could practise for hours, the dusk drawing down, light leaking from the hall through holes in the clapboard sides, moths blurring in the pencils of brightness. People often stopped to listen as they passed on the street beyond, the gravel cracking beneath their feet when they ventured further towards the hall to hear more clearly the drums and flutes, Bingham's barked instructions sounding small against the torrent of sound.

We listened out for these passers-by, the crackle of the plastic shopping bags in their hands, the muttered comments they made to one another, praise for the music and the return of the marching season coming to us in those moments of clear silence that escaped from the music, when the Cooke boys took a breath and the sticks in Bingham's fists struck air.

Then one evening we heard somebody come most of the way down the path, between the nasturtium beds planted to burst into orange flower by the end of June. We heard him stop for a while, his breathing fast and coarse, as though he had been running. We retreated as far back into the shadows as we could for fear that he might come around to the side of the hall where we were hiding, our arms knitting together, each of us recognizing the tremor of fear in the other. Whoever it was stood on the gravel for a few minutes, and all that time we silently willed them to go on into the hall or leave.

The noise on the galvanized roof of the hall was sudden, as if something had fallen from the sky, and our hearts leapt. I stood up and made to run, but Catherine grabbed my ankle and pulled me down.

'They'll see you!' she whispered as the thrown gravel tumbled down off the roof and fell into our hair, ticking on our bare arms and legs, falling soundlessly into the grass and nettles.

When we looked around we saw him, turning at the gate, the familiar bald spot on his crown, the faintest smudge of light against the side of his face that darkened to beard.

Seamus.

The drumming stopped first, then the fifes trailed

away to nothing. We heard Bingham's heavy tread across the floorboards and watched the oblong of light thrown out across the gravel path as the front door was opened. Bingham came down the steps and looked around, the Lambeg sitting proud on his stomach, the sticks gripped tightly on either side, his sleeves rolled up to his elbows. We could hear his panting, the drum weighing on him, his chest heaving. He slowly made his way back up the steps, kicking the door shut behind him in silent anger.

'I know who you are!' Bingham roared out into the dark. His spit caught in the light as it flew from his lips like venom. Then he hissed in a quiet voice which was all the more menacing for the fact that it could barely be heard, 'We'll fix you yet, you dirty little Taig fucker. I'll have the boys fix you good and proper as soon as I get the chance.'

'What was it?' we heard Mr Cooke ask, his voice trembling as it always did, as if he was in constant fear of being struck by something unexpected.

'Taigs was all it was,' Bingham spat. 'Taigs with nothing better to do than annoy those with work to be done. We'll show them on the Twelfth, won't we, boys?'

'Aye, Mr Bingham,' the Cooke boys chimed in unison, and the fifes were lifted to their lips again, the notes entwined with the drum beats.

*

When we saw Seamus the following evening he looked
no different, the bottles of Guinness opened one after
the other as always after an afternoon's work with Da,
the tick of the metal caps on the sideboard reminding
me of the tick of the gravel he had thrown onto the
roof. I watched his face as the second cap fell but it
meant nothing to him, only the lips parting in satisfac-
tion at the malted drink that was to come, the creamy
froth curving into the bottom of the tilted glass. The
chairs creaked under their weight as they sat back,
glasses in hand.

'Aye,' Da sighed.

'God b-bless now,' Seamus said, raising his glass.

It had been a hot day, the first of that summer,
the workshop windows pushed open, the paint flaking
away to reveal scales of brown rust.

When I came in from school, always through the
arch and into the well of the yard, the air would be
filled with the sweet smell of sap from whatever wood
had been cut that day: beech, willow, ash. And still the
onset of summer is tethered for me to that timber smell,
even though it is many, many years since Da's saw
stopped its spinning, the workshop's metal windows
sealed for good, frames rotting to nothing and never
replaced.

The smell of cut timber hung in the front room that
evening too, mixed with the malt of the beer and the

faintest edge of lavender from the drawer where Ma kept the table linen.

'Hello, Catherine,' Seamus greeted when she came in from the kitchen. 'How did you get on in school today?'

Catherine stared at him and then at me. She was trying to match the features of the fleeing figure from the night before with those of the uncle who sat in the chair, swilling stout around the bottom of his glass, froth snagged in the edge of his moustache.

'Have you lost your tongue?' Da asked. 'Will you not answer your Uncle Seamus?'

She looked at me but I turned away, finding through the white mesh of curtain a narrowing blade of light on the red brick of the houses opposite. It travelled the façades, picking out the white painted window and door frames, the thick black downpipes, the dull sheen of engineering brick.

All that time I felt her eyes upon my face. Even on our journey back along the Ways the night before we had not spoken of it, our feet counting out the steps home, superstition making us careful to avoid the glow where house lights cast ghosts onto the flags. It had weighed between us, as still it weighed, unspoken for fear of what it might mean.

'No, Da,' Catherine broke. 'I was daydreaming. Sorry.'

'What harm?' Seamus said. 'What harm? D-Don't

we all need to have our d-dreams, don't we?' He looked from Catherine to Da, smiling.

Over dinner we watched Seamus, as if something about the way he ate could tell us more.

'Aren't you away to the darts at all, Seamus?' Ma asked when we were all finished and the clearing away had begun.

'I'm away this m-minute.'

'Go on or I'll sweep the ground from beneath you.' She laughed, putting her hand on the broom that stood inside the door. 'Go on!' She pushed the brush up against his boots.

'I know when I'm not w-wanted.' Seamus smiled with mock offence, turning out into the hall. He called his goodbyes to Da, who was in the toilet. The front door closed suddenly shut behind Seamus, catching a draught from the street outside, leaving an exaggerated silence in his wake.

After the table had been cleared and the plates and cutlery washed and dried, we joined Ma in the front room. She turned on the radiogram. Music was playing, soft and tinny, like jazz, the signal alive with static.

'I remember this!' Ma smiled, putting her hands together in a clap that made no sound. Slowly she began to dance, the merest switching of her hips to the music, her feet shuffling along the carpet. Her eyes were barely open and her face was tilted upwards as though sunlight was falling through the black miles of night and caressing her.

We woke the next morning to find the day slicked with mist, Catherine's hopscotch marks puddled like milk on the flagstones. Ma had hoped for the dry weather to continue so that the hen's feet would not get the canker that rose from the cobbles to lodge between the scales on their ankles.

I spent most of the afternoon idly looking for Catherine. The rhododendrons on the railway embankment spilled warm rainwater onto me when I searched for her there, but our patch of grass held only snails and rabbit droppings. None of her schoolfriends had seen her. When I asked the boy who waited all day for customers on the sand with two saddled donkeys, he just shrugged his shoulders. At the Orange Hall I stood on the front wall and peered across towards our hiding place, but only wasps came and went from the crates of bottles. I ran home along the Ways, calling her name at every crossing point, kicking a Pepsi can between the back walls of the houses.

The smell from the workshop where Da and Seamus were cutting long lengths of deal for a fence seemed richer and thicker, the sap drawn out to meet the moisture in the air. Seamus had a knack of judging exactly how much to add on to each length to compensate for the humidity, so that on a drier day the boards would still fit perfectly.

'D'you see now, young M-Michael?' he said, pointing to his tongue.

I looked at the thick, grey-furred muscle, a curious blue stain like a question mark lurking beneath the surface. His tongue quivered above his teeth, the tip searching like a mouse's snout.

I shook my head.

'Well now,' Seamus jawed. 'If that t-tongue is still wet after fifteen seconds, I'll add an extra sixth of an inch to every b-board. If it's dry after ten then we're fine and d-dandy with what we have. And if it's dry after five, then I'll take a sliver off the end for g-good luck.'

'Right,' I said.

'But let me tell you now,' he continued. 'I could count on the f-fingers of one hand the times I've had to take a fraction off on account of the day being so d-dry.'

'Aye,' Da agreed. 'We're forever adding on, and that blasted timber merchant won't shave a shilling off his prices, no matter how much business we put his way.'

'Oh, and you can be sure his own kind are getting the b-best timber and the b-best prices,' Seamus said, heaving another length onto the bench.

Da glared at him. He never welcomed these comments, especially when he was working. He wouldn't want an argument to start that might distract them from whatever they were working on.

'Well, it's t-true, isn't it?' Seamus challenged.

Da spun the handle on the vice to lock a timber in place. The wood squeaked and Da cursed under his breath.

'I'll go on all right, Seamus,' Da sighed. 'I'll go on with the young lad into the house. I'm fierce tired the day, to tell you the truth.'

'Aye,' Seamus said. 'Go on so. I'll carry on with these fellas for a while yet.'

Da took his jacket and slung it over his shoulder. He said nothing on his way out of the door. Behind us the saw started up again, to and fro, to and fro.

'Go out to the workshop like a good lad and fetch your Uncle Seamus,' Da said later, when he had settled into the armchair in the front room, uncapping the bottles of Guinness and filling a glass for himself. He would never fill Seamus's glass, and neither would he want his own filled in his absence. 'Tell him the stout will be gone stale if he's not in soon.'

'Aye,' I said, turning away from the window, where the rain had just ceased, the boot prints of two men who had passed still greyly visible on the wet flags: wide, curved grooves – factory workers.

From the hallway I could hear Ma setting places for dinner, the cutlery wiped with a glass cloth before being laid out, the pewter condiment set that swung in a wire cage from a cradle moved to the centre of the table.

'Will you call Catherine, wherever she is?' Ma said when I came through the door.

As the last word left her mouth a shot rang out in the back yard.

In the sudden silence after that first shot I watched Ma's hand slowly reaching for the table. There were two more shots then, so close together that they seemed one, but afterwards everyone who had heard them said they were separate. Ma's hand slipped across the table and the cradle tipped over, salt and pepper trickling into neat piles on the gingham-patterned oil cloth.

She was looking at me. I lifted my hands to my ears, but when no more shots came I took them away again. Da was running through the hallway behind me.

'Where's Catherine?' he gasped, pushing me to one side, his eyes frantically searching the square of yard framed in the window where the hens were going crazy, as if a fox had been set loose among them.

Da was out of the back door in a flash and I could see the very top of his head through the window, bobbing towards the workshop. When I made to follow him Ma caught my shirt and pulled me back.

'No!' she breathed, drawing me to her, the serving spoons she still held pressing into my ribs. I could feel her chest heaving at my back, the stiff folds of her apron against my neck. 'Seamus!' she said suddenly, as if everything that had happened in those seconds could be condensed into his name.

She let go of me and went to the window, the serving spoons clattering down into the sink. I watched her lift herself up on tiptoes to see more of the yard, her nose almost touching the glass.

When I got to the back door there was a silence and a waiting in the yard, as if something had started and swollen into it, pushing the hens back into their house, where their throats hummed and purred like small, idling engines. Da was slumped on the cobbles at the open door to the workshop, his elbows resting on his knees, hands pressed across his ears as if somebody was whispering something terrible to him from within the depths of the workshop.

Ma went to him and stood with her hand on his shoulder. Between them I could see the soles of Seamus's work boots, flecked with wood shavings and sharp stones pressed into the leather. A hen emerged and went across to the workshop door, cocking its head to one side to observe them.

'No! Ah, no!' Ma screamed, stepping across his feet and disappearing into the workshop.

Da reached for her, his fingers grabbing the knotted cord of her apron which unravelled in his hand, much as in later years the grief of never knowing would cause the knot of their own lives to unravel.

10 London

Soon it will be time to leave. The house is coming apart. Gaps are beginning to appear between the walls and the ceiling and the doors are sticking on their hinges so that they have to be shouldered open and shut. Loose mortar trickles into unseen spaces. The plumbing is being wrenched asunder. When I lie on my bed in the boxroom, which it is now my turn to have, I can hear timbers shuddering and creaking, the joists inching apart. I imagine row upon row of nail heads pushing up from the floorboards.

In the staff room all the talk is of the summer break. Elaine Grimm is hiring some of the classrooms for the arts and crafts summer school she runs during July. The two teachers who joined in September are travelling around Europe together on a rail pass. Mead has elected to correct examination papers, the weeks of summer spent as ever among the figures and lines that are his first and only love.

Frances finds me at the window, vacantly gazing down at the heads of the children in the schoolyard far below.

I haven't seen her for some days. She looks prettier than ever, perhaps because not seeing her has made me more aware of how beautiful she is. With the warmer weather she is wearing brighter colours that light up her smooth and perfect skin. The sun has thrown a splash of the faintest freckles across her nose. There are flints of silver in the irises of her eyes. As we talk I wonder what it would be like to kiss her mouth, to feel the coolness of those lips on mine.

'What will you do for summer?' I ask.

'I'll probably go home to Dublin to keep my mother company. We'll potter in the garden together. Go to the theatre, have lunch in the National Gallery.'

'It wouldn't do to stay in London, then?'

'Oh, God, no. The last thing she asked me before I came over here was to promise to visit her every Christmas, Easter and summer. With her having bought the flat for me it would seem unfair not to go.' She puts her hand against the window and looks down at the children.

'London is the best city in the world during summer,' I offer. 'You'd like it here.'

'I'm sure I would,' she sighs. Her hand moves slowly

across her face, as if to smooth away wrinkles that aren't there.

The waters of the canal are so still that the buildings along the towpath look like they have been unfolded from their reflections, like a child's pop-up book. When I look at Frances I see the honey and orange light from the buildings in her eyes. I look away again. The other teachers' conversation seems hugely distant.

'It looks like it'll be a nice evening for a drink,' I begin.

'OK.'

'OK, what?'

'OK, I'll join you.' She smiles. When she blinks, the reflected buildings disappear and appear again.

'I never . . .' I protest.

'OK, then, I won't.'

'What?'

She breaks out laughing. 'The look on your face! You'd swear you were about to lose your life. Of course I'd love to go for a drink.'

The bell above the door rings and the conversation behind us suddenly rises then falls away again as we prepare for the afternoon classes and the hours that will take me to meet her again.

'This is a lovely spot,' Frances says when we turn into the pub on Compton Avenue, squares of rich evening sun lazing on the worn burgundy carpet and the bare wood tables and benches. A Labrador is asleep in the cool of the foot well at the bar and I think of the stationmaster's dog circling the platform for shade on summer afternoons in Portnew. 'Who told you about it?' Frances asks. 'It'd be impossible to find otherwise.'

'I came across it on one of the walks I used to take during my first months here,' I say. 'Walking is a great way of getting to know a place.'

'You must have covered every square inch of the town, then.' She laughs. Her charcoal cotton dress is sleeveless and pinched at the waist before flaring out into perfect rows of pleats. The whorl of an inoculation mark sits on her upper arm, the only blemish I can find. Her back is narrow, the ridges of shoulder blades moving under the fabric when she stoops to find some change in her handbag.

As we talk, the squares of sun move slowly across us, motes of dust lingering undisturbed in the shafts of light. The landlord sits on a stool at the far end of the bar, smoking and chatting to another man who is standing with his back to the wall, a pint of bitter cradled against his chest. The landlord is leaning in towards the bar, seeming to gaze into the sink, while the other man's eyes appear to be tracing the ceiling covings. I always enjoy seeing them like this, seeming not to be talking at all, the language of their bodies all wrong, but the air between them is thick with conversation.

When Frances laughs she tilts her head back so that the smooth lines of her throat show, the tendons drawn taut beneath the almond silk of her skin. Her pulse flutters there like the heart of a bird, tiny as an orange seed.

'And you won't be going home for summer?' she asks, her mouth and nose looking swollen through the heavy glass bottom of the glass, like the face of an underwater explorer framed in a diving bell.

'I might pay a wee visit, but I never stay with the folks for long. I'll take a walk in the Mourne Mountains if the weather is halfway decent, which it rarely is. The Silent Valley can be great if you catch it right. The views are tremendous so long as Newcastle doesn't get in the way – it reminds me too much of home.'

'I've never been,' she says, draining her glass. 'I've heard, though, that it's just like Bray, outside Dublin.'

'Aye, it is,' I say, rising to go to the bar.

'I'll get this one,' she says.

I watch her at the bar, smoothing her hair behind her ears before looking for the barman's attention. She puts her feet perfectly together on the footrail and lifts herself ever so slightly while she waits for the stout to settle in the glasses. The landlord says something to her as he takes the change she offers and her shoulders shake when she laughs. He smiles at her.

A few dry leaves blow in the open door and crackle under her feet as she brings the drinks back. When she smiles the sunlight catches the flints in her eyes and they sparkle. Her face lights up. She leans on my knee when she goes to sit back down. A warmth spreads through me. She is sitting closer to me now and everything seems newly possible. I look at her hand where it rests upon the edge of the table, skin against the grain.

The pub is beginning to fill up and the landlord's wife has come out to help behind the bar. The offices and shops are closing for the night, the workers escaping to the bars to enjoy the warmth and ease of the long evening, the last blue fading in the sky beyond the trees and roofs.

When a group of people asks Frances to move along to make room for them she shuffles up the bench against me. We joke with the others about the possibility of sitting on the table as well as the benches. I can feel the tremor in her when she laughs.

We exchange stories about our first school year and the mistakes we each made at the outset. For every embarrassing classroom incident I recall, Frances produces an even more embarrassing one.

'Come on,' she starts a little while later when our drinks are finished.

At Canonbury Square she stops to wonder at the tall houses where lights have begun to come on in the great front rooms and hallways, the stucco plasterwork of the ceilings thrown into sharp relief, brasswork gleaming on the doors. In one of the houses a woman is going from room to room closing the window shutters, pausing to look down at the street as she does.

'Do you think she minds having people staring at her house like this?' Frances asks.

'I'd say she's become so used to it by now that she no longer notices.'

'Imagine living in a house as wonderful as that, though,' she sighs. 'To have a home like that over-looking a square of trees and flowers, and to have this view at the end of each day. Wouldn't it be just perfect?'

'Aye,' I say. 'But who knows what goes on behind those shutters? She might have a husband who no longer loves her, or who is always at work. Perhaps she is looking out in the hope that someone lost will return,' I say.

I think of my own mother, vigilant in her armchair behind the window of our terraced house in Portnew, her eyes always on the street, the way she talks about the hopscotch marks that Catherine used to chalk on the pavements and that have been washed away by years of rain. Ma sees them still on every kerbstone, bending double to trace their lost outlines with the tip of her finger, calling out for Da or a neighbour to lift her when arthritis locks her knees and she can no longer straighten.

'Why would you think that?' Frances asks. She slips her hand into the crook of my elbow and gives a little shiver that is like an electric current to me. 'That's the strangest thing to say.'

At the end of the terrace of houses the pavement descends to the street in a row of steps and she leans into me as we go down. 'Stranger things happen than are ever said,' I say.

'Do you know what else is strange?' she says, drawing to a halt.

'What?'

'I was married once.'

'Married?' I feel my heart sinking and everything around me growing suddenly cold. 'You've never said.'

'It was a while ago. We were only married for a couple of years. We got married to save ourselves. We hoped it wouldn't end but it was over long before we realized.'

'I'm sorry, Frances. It must have been very difficult.'

'It would have been more difficult had we not admitted to ourselves that it was over,' she says, sweeping her hair back behind her eyes.

'Where is he now?' I ask.

'Believe it or not,' she shrugs, 'I don't have a notion. We went separately to collect our things from the house we rented. Everything I owned fitted into a couple of suitcases – it wasn't much after two years together, but it made things easier, I suppose.'

'And you never heard from him again?' I cannot imagine how people who had shared so much would never again hear from each other, that the intimacy they had once had could count for so little, could mean absolutely nothing.

Frances shakes her head. 'It's like it never happened.'

She turns her face to mine and I see the glisten of her lips, her hair that is now muddled but still perfectly frames her face. Her eyes look into mine for a moment and it feels like they are needles. Her pupils flicker as if she is searching for something in me. My mouth goes dry and everything seems about to change when her lips reach towards mine and we kiss. I breathe her in, the other scent of her, her skin, her hair. Our lips barely touch. I can feel her breath in my mouth.

She pulls away a little and sighs and lifts her face towards the first stars of the night. I bend to kiss the arch of her throat, the cool and smooth skin I find there. When my tongue flickers into the socket above her breastbone I hear her saying no and no and no.

'Michael,' she says, lifting my face away from her.

'What?'

'Isn't this strange?'

'No,' I say. 'It isn't strange at all.' When I try to pull her back to me she steps away. Her neck glistens where I have kissed her. 'What's wrong?'

'This is wrong. I'm sorry, it's wrong.'

'Why? How?'

'It feels wrong.'

Her fingers are at her lips and then at her neck, as if, waking from a dream, she is checking to see if it was real. Her eyes are wide open, half startled. 'I'm sorry,' she says, her breath quickening. 'I don't want to hurt you but I can't do this.'

'Why not? Don't you like it . . . me?'

'Yes, yes, of course I do, but it's too soon, far too soon.'

'Since . . . since *him*? Is that it?'

She nods, tears wetting her eyes.

'I hope you don't think I've forced you into anything you don't want,' I say.

She shakes her head and sweeps the hair back off her forehead and clenches it with her fist against her scalp. 'I'm sorry,' she says, and touches my wrist, but when I go to take her hand she turns away. 'Can I get a taxi from there?' she asks suddenly, pointing to a junction that is busy with cars and buses.

'Yes, but I'll take you home,' I say.

'There's no need for that, Michael. I can make my own way.' She sweeps her hair behind her ears and straightens herself.

'At least let me walk you to the taxi.'

'OK,' she agrees, and we walk down the curving hill where the lights of the old dockyards are visible above the rooftops. While the traffic hums past and buses draw up then away again, I look sideways at Frances, who is searching the street for the orange light of an empty taxi. I think of those few minutes when we kissed. It seems like something that happened a long time ago, when we were different people. Everything has changed since then, even the night has grown cool. I had wanted to kiss her, to touch her, to hold her and to begin to close over the holes in each of our lives.

She calls out and waves her raised arm when she sees a taxi. It pulls to a halt a little way up the street. She hurries past me.

'I'll see you in the morning, then?' I ask as she bends into the back of the taxi, but she does not answer. I watch her giving directions to the driver, her mouth moving with the words behind the glass just as I have often watched her addressing her pupils through the rectangle of safety glass in the classroom door. I imagine the lilt of her voice and the driver asking her where she is from as he signals and pulls out into the stream of traffic, the throbbing of the diesel engine as he bears her away until the lights of her taxi are lost among all of the others and dissolved in the night of the city.

11 Portnew

'Tell me what you saw, Catherine. Please.'

There was no answer, my question hanging about us in the dark of the bedroom we now shared, so that should she wake with night terrors she would not be alone.

'Catherine, *please*.'

I listened to the rasp of her breathing. The room was so small that from where I lay I could touch her mattress. John O'Connell, a fitter's apprentice from two doors up, had taken her bed apart and moved it into my bedroom, marvelling at the way the boards slotted together to form a solid frame, the complete lack of movement once the metal bolts had been fastened into place.

'Your Da's a wizard with wood,' he had praised as I took a spanner from the tool bag and handed it to him.

They had found Catherine up on the old hayloft in

the workshop half an hour after Seamus had been shot, curled up so tightly that they were able to lift her down without her ever moving a muscle. The two fingers she had stuffed into her mouth to stifle her screams were still in place when they carried her into the kitchen.

Ma leaned over her, cradling her head against her chest, whispering in her ear, the words 'love' and 'safe' repeated over and over again.

'Are you still awake, Catherine?' I reached across and put the flat of my palm against the mattress and felt the shivering of her body, the tightened breathing as she tried to hold everything in. 'Why won't you tell?'

I only knew what I had seen in the yard.

A police officer had stood for a couple of hours beneath the archway with a length of white tape stretched between a pair of kitchen chairs at the workshop door. But it was the chalk outlines of boot prints on the cobbles leading from the archway to the workshop and back again which had fascinated me the most. The officer had marked the prints out before they dried and were lost, his boots creaking as he bent to trace the outlines. I thought of Catherine's hopscotch grids on the street outside.

At the workshop door another chalk circle marked where a bullet casing had rolled, the dull gold-coloured metal shining grimly from between two broken cobbles. As I had turned to look inside the workshop one of my sneakers squeaked on a wet cobble and I froze, waiting for the officer standing guard beneath the arch to swing around and find me there. I could feel the blood rising to my head and a buzzing in my ears, but he didn't turn around.

Just inside the door were another two chalk circles where more bullet casings had dropped, and there, among the usual shavings, parings and sawdust, were the pools of dark blood where Seamus had fallen, the bow saw he had been holding lying half buried in a pile of sawdust. His blood had dried to the colour of molasses, soaking into the shavings and parings so that they showed dark and black against the brightness of those that remained untouched. Otherwise the workshop was as it always was, the tools waiting on their hooks fixed to the wall, the blades of chisels glimmering like rectangles of light thrown by an unseen window. Even the wooden ladder with which they had removed Catherine from the hayloft had been returned to its place behind the door.

I had peered up into that close and darkened space where she had lain and watched as so often before she had watched Da and Seamus going about their work. The white tape across the doorway stopped me from going any further, and in any case I did not want to set foot in there, nor stand in the gloom where Seamus had once stood. There was a new hollowness in there now, something carved out between all of us who had known him.

I moved between sleep and empty wondering all through that night, listening to the strain of Catherine's breathing like a parent listening to an infant. There were times when I was sure she was awake and I would sit up in the bed and ask her what she had seen time and again; and always that same silence, the pale skin like candle wax in the twilit phrase of moonlight seeping through the curtain to fall upon her forehead, her cheeks, her sometimes shut sometimes open eyes, the curving intrigue of her mouth.

'Da!' I called from my bedroom window the next morning. 'Da!'

He came out of the workshop and looked up at me, shielding his eyes with his hand. His cheeks were glazed with sweat, like Ma's were with tears. 'Aye!' His voice sounded thin and reedy, wheezing with effort.

'I'll help you with the bags up to the pet shop, Da!' I said, leaning out as far as I could so that I wouldn't have to shout.

He smiled weakly and looked down at his boots for a moment. 'They're not going to the pet shop at all, son.'

'Where are they going, then?'

'I'll tell you later.'

'Are the police taking them away, is that it, Da?'

He shook his head. 'Go on inside now.'

Da went out with the bags and returned an hour later, just as the Lambegs began.

He went to sit in the front room, but as soon as he had opened his bottle he stood up again to pour it. There was a smell of smoke from his clothes, sweet like burnt leaves or paper.

'Where did you bring the bags, Da?'

'I burned them up at the quarry,' he said tiredly.

'Burned them?'

'Aye.'

'Why did you burn them, Da?'

He spun around, taking one step towards me and leaning his face into mine. 'I burned them, Michael, because I wanted rid of them,' he roared. 'I burned them because your poor uncle's blood was among them.' He grabbed my shoulders and shook me hard. 'Do you hear me now, do you?'

I felt the heat in my eyes spilling over like a boiled kettle, the tears running down my face as they had not run since Seamus had been killed, the curious wonder at his death and the manner of it suddenly lifted and gone. I felt my sobbing beating out into that room with its catalogues of the living and the dead that Seamus would soon join, and Da standing before me, cautiously watching, his hands upon my shoulders.

'Michael?' His voice threaded its way through my crying, thin and distant, as if it was lost in the dryness of his throat and mouth and could come no further.

Through the glaze of tears I saw him swallow, his Adam's apple moving slow as a diving bell. 'I'm sorry I shouted at you, son,' he whispered. 'I lost the run of myself for a bit.' He squeezed my shoulders as I had seen him squeezing Ma's. 'I'm sorry,' he said again.

Beyond the room I heard a door opening and someone stepping from the kitchen into the hallway. It was Ma, her weight causing a board that Da must have missed to creak minutely. He made a ticking sound in the roof of his mouth when he heard it.

Da drew me to him and hugged me. He smelled of burning mixed with the sweat from dragging the bags up the hill. He turned away when the door eased open but there was nothing there, just the emptiness of the framed space where I had expected Ma to be. She had returned to the kitchen and the draught had pushed open the door. Da scrubbed his hand through my hair and went out to her, moving stiffly as though the ache in his heart had spread to his limbs. I listened to their voices in the kitchen for a while, Da explaining why he had shouted and Ma telling him that it was all right.

The dark boards for Seamus's coffin hid Da from view as he wheeled them up the street on a trolley he had borrowed from the coal yard. The wheels of the trolley squeaked, the noise drawing some of the neighbours to their doors. They made the sign of the cross and turned away before Da could see them, the doors quietly clicking shut again, one by one.

I watched Da wheel the boards in under the arch and across the cobbles to the workshop door. He spent all afternoon working on them, the whirr of the mechanical saw cutting through the stillness in the yard. He emerged just the once to hurry off down to the town, returning with a large cardboard box. Somehow I knew not to go out to him.

At dusk he was still in the workshop. Ma brought his dinner out to him, her face filled with tears when she returned to the kitchen, where we ate in silence. Much later, I lay in bed and listened to the steady thrum of the Coronet lathe, its bearings spinning in their bath of warm oil, the short buzz as a chisel blade was pushed against a piece of wood, and then the tapping of Da's hammer like a bird calling out in the black night.

12 London

We have not spoken for days. It seems an age since that single kiss and yet it is no more than two weeks ago. That kiss has changed everything and now she seems locked behind glass.

This is our last week together and once the exams are finished we will all go our separate ways. Like every senior class that I have taught, the children are bored at the prospect of the end of what they claim to be the most boring years of their lives. They appear to have no plans for the months and years ahead and are prepared to let their lives take their own course.

When the bell goes the students slowly gather their books and shuffle out of the door. The blackboard is empty. There is nothing left to teach. A saw starts up in the timber yard across the canal, a high buzzing sound that changes with the grain of the wood, screeching at every knot then falling quickly away as the timber parts.

'Hi there, Michael.' Her voice slips around the bare classroom walls.

When I turn around Frances is standing in the frame of the doorway, one foot inside the classroom. She is smiling.

'Sorry, did I give you a fright?'

'No, no. I was gazing out of the window, that's all.'

She comes across to the window and has to stand on tiptoes to see above the frosted panes. Her fingers are like narrow candles where she has pressed them upon the dark wood of the windowsill to lift herself up. Her nails are painted a deep blood red that I have not seen her wear before. I can smell her perfume amidst the stale classroom smell of chalk and paper and clothes.

'The timber yard must remind you of your father,' she says. 'Does he have a yard like that back home?'

'Oh, no.' I laugh. 'No bigger than this classroom, but when I was a wean it seemed the biggest place in the world. He doesn't work there any more, mind.'

'No? Why not?'

'Well, things happened. Ach, it's a long story,' I say. 'I'll tell you another time.'

She looks into my face, then quickly looks away again. 'I'm sorry that I've been ignoring you, Michael,' she begins. 'It's just . . .'

'I'm sorry too,' I say.

'You've nothing to be sorry about,' she insists. She curls a few strands of hair around her finger and then rests her other hand on the back of mine. She thumps me lightly on the chest and laughs. 'So here we are then, apologizing to each other over nothing.'

'I know,' I say, and I turn my hand around to take hers, the painted fingernails that look so livid upon my palm.

The saw in the timber yard comes to a sudden halt and the classroom seems even emptier than before.

'We wouldn't want anyone to see us,' she says, glancing across at the half-open door. 'Why don't we go for something to eat?'

'Aye, why not?'

When she turns around she brushes against me and I can smell the sweetness of her hair and something like electricity passes between us.

The street near her flat is buzzing with people. The evening air is heavy with herbs and spices: cardamom, coriander, garam masala, garlic, chilli peppers, nutmeg, ginger. The restaurant Frances recommends is full, a line of couples already waiting in the narrow doorway, the proprietor murmuring his apologies for the delay and encouraging us to return later. We move from window to window, examining the menus and peering through the curtains to gauge the atmosphere. Some restaurants are full and others almost completely empty, waiters strolling around the vacant tables, a host venturing onto the street to encourage us inside. When we return to the place that Frances recommended the proprietor is surprised to see us but shakes our hands and shows us to a row of raised booths at the far end of the restaurant where webs of shadow are thrown by bamboo screens. The tables are low, as if designed for infants.

'Is this OK?' Frances asks, stepping out of her shoes and folding her legs beneath her so that she can squat at the table.

'Aye, sure it is,' I say, crouching at the other side.

Frances's feet are long and slender with high arches that scoop down to her toenails, which are painted a pale pink. I can see the bones moving when she reaches across for another poppadom. I want to take her foot in my hand and feel the mechanics of those bones and tendons like the wing of a bird against my palm.

A waiter appears with our starters laid out in stainless-steel bowls and plates, and Frances tells me what to mix with what, the combination of taste and textures that are new to me.

Frances eats slowly, small parcels of food knifed onto her fork or folded into pieces of naan bread, her painted lips barely parting to eat.

'Why did you come over?' she asks.

I don't know what to say. Every table around us seems to have descended into silence, as if they too are waiting for me to answer. I drink some beer to clear my mouth and give me time. Frances looks at me, her fingers moulding a piece of bread, thinking.

'For work really, aye,' I say, 'and to get away from things.'

'From the Troubles, you mean?' Like every Southerner, Frances hesitates a little when she mentions the Troubles in the North, as if acknowledging a personal bereavement, her voice lowering and stiffening.

'Aye, them too.'

The proprietor returns to our booth to ask us if we are enjoying our meal and to light the candle in the yellow glass bowl between us. It burns sweetly and a few moments later the restaurant lights are dimmed, a candle aflame on every table, faces thrown to masks of shadow, the hum of conversation gone to the rustle of whispering.

'What else was there?' Frances asks.

I pour the rest of the Indian beer and watch the bands of froth rocking towards the rims of our glasses.

'My uncle was shot,' I say simply. His smile returns to me, his stammer, the fat pink freckles that appeared on his forearms in summer: Uncle Seamus.

Frances lifts a hand to her mouth. 'I'm sorry,' she says. 'I'm sorry.'

'Ach, it was a long time ago now. I wasn't much more than a wean at the time.'

Frances lifts her head and leans towards me. 'You've

never mentioned it before,' she says, a sort of sorrow cracking in her voice.

'Nobody from the North ever mentions those things. It doesn't help to go over them again but sometimes you just can't help it.'

'Oh, Michael, it must have been terrible for you.'

'I suppose it was, aye, but my Ma's never got over it. He was her brother and they shot him in our back yard. She says she still sees him lying there every time she looks out of the kitchen window.'

I remember seeing Seamus's work boots pointing towards the sky and the hen cocking its head to look inside the workshop.

Frances casts her eyes down, trapping her lip in her teeth. There is pity in her face. 'Your poor mother,' she says.

'They were close,' I say, the sound of their laughing on that evening when she shooed him from the kitchen with her broom returning to me. 'We were his family – he hadn't married.'

'I've heard that every family has lost someone in the Troubles.'

'If you live in Twinbrook, Bogside, Shankill or the Falls that might be true. They're in the middle of it, but Portnew is in the middle of nowhere. It's only a wee town and no one else was killed there before or since. A few beatings and hoax bombs maybe, and I remember an incendiary device burning a shelf of toys in

Wellworths, but little else. When I was a youngster I felt left out of it all, but after Seamus was killed I was grateful for it.'

Frances puts her hand across mine, as someone might momentarily do to offer their sympathy, but she leaves it there, the warmth of her palm folded across my knuckles, which are chapped with chalk. I feel the same tremble in her as in myself. When I look into her face her eyes are on our joined hands, the lids half unfolded, her skin smooth as china. The candle moulds light across her face, showing her cheekbones, the ridge of her nose, the dip that funnels between her nose and upper lip, where Catherine's scar had run. When she breathes her nostrils flare just a little. Her eyelashes flicker. A pulse beats in her neck, to and fro, to and fro.

'I'm sorry about your uncle,' she says.

'I know that. It was a long time ago now.'

She lifts her eyes to look at me. Her pupils are wide open and in them I can see the dark shape of my face among a circle of lights from the tables ranged behind me.

'Will we get the bill?' she says. I watch her mouth making the words. Her hand does not move from mine.

I call the waiter over and he brings the bill a couple of minutes later. When the proprietor shows us out of the door, there is a small queue of people on the pavement outside.

When I take Frances's hand in mine she makes no

attempt to shrug it off but there is no strength in her grip either, her fingers folding limply in mine. The street-lamps light her face then throw it back into darkness as we walk, our shadows seeming to revolve beneath us. Televisions flicker in front windows all along her street. The shapes of people can be seen moving behind curtains.

When I put my arm around her shoulder she blinks and tilts her head towards mine. I can feel her warmth against my face.

A magnolia tree standing over the steps to her house is in dull leaf, the plain grey-green leaves a disappointment after the satin luxury of the earlier blossoms.

The hallway echoes of dead letters, broken umbrellas, dry leaves and Bakelite switches. The wallpaper is old, a brown pattern of interlocking squares that is broken up by work that has been done over the years to install telephone lines, electricity and gas meters, water pipes, rewiring. A wooden Formica-topped table holds a jar of dried teasels, their spines broken and scattered to the floor like pine needles.

When she opens the door of her flat and throws on the light she turns suddenly around. She opens her mouth to say something and there is a tremor of breath but no words come.

'What's wrong?' I ask, taking her hand, which hangs limply in mine.

She shakes her head then turns into the flat.

The living-room walls are pale yellow, the wood-work painted white. A cane sofa is pushed into one corner and two tall bookcases rise on either side of the hearth, over which a square mirror is hung. The bookcases are filled with the orange and black spines of Penguin paperbacks, travel books and a few hardback novels. A blue Matisse print hangs on the wall behind the sofa. The floorboards have been stripped bare and honey-glazed with varnish.

There is little in her flat that does not need to be there, everything is as it should be, and yet as I move through its rooms with her there is a lingering empti-ness, as if her life is not lived here at all, but elsewhere.

'Well,' she says. 'That's the end of the grand tour, such as it is.'

'It's a lovely place you have here,' I say, smiling. 'You keep it well.'

When she brings a bottle of wine into the living room she switches on a couple of lamps and turns off the ceiling light so that the light lowers and softens. Through the window the shapes of the plane trees in the street outside can be seen against the night sky. She tells me about the area, about other flats she saw before she decided on this one, how she only found it when she went to look at an inferior flat next door.

'You were lucky, then,' I say.

'There is luck in everything,' she sighs, lifting her wine glass onto her lap and folding her legs under her. Her arm hangs limply between us and when I take her wrist she swallows and her lips part a little. Her wrist is impossibly narrow, the skin so tender that it might never have seen the sun, a mesh of tendon, vein and artery that I trace first with my finger and then my lips.

When I go to unbutton her dress she hesitates for a moment and looks into my face. She lets out a string of small gasps when I undo her bra and take her breasts in my hands, as if, one by one, I am drawing pebbles from her mouth.

'We should go to the bedroom,' she whispers a little while later when I go to hitch her dress up to her waist.

'Aye,' I say, taking her hand.

When I lie on the bed she turns off the lamp so that the only light is that of a streetlamp filtering through the leaves of a copper beech, a frame of them fallen like scales across the sheets.

Across her breastbone, where her flesh seems gossamer-thin, is laid a map of veins, barely blue, so faint that they seem hardly capable of their task. With the tip of my tongue I trace the topography of her, spreading her skin between my thumbs to reveal layer upon layer of vein and capillary. All the time she is moving so gently beneath me, her fingers finding the spaces between the vertebrae of my spine, pressing on the bones there like piano keys.

As I enter her she fixes my eyes with hers, her mouth

opening and closing with every motion, her fingers spread across my shoulders, her breath held for what seems an eternity until the suddenness of that final release.

Afterwards she lies folded in my arms. We talk about nothing for a while: the play of the leaf shadows across the bed, the weekend that is just now beginning, laughing when our conversation turns inevitably towards the summer that is ahead of us. She falls easily to sleep. I lie awake, watching her face on the pillow, her features, which in sleep are no less perfect than in waking, the dark tangle of her hair upon the pillow, the symmetry of the ridges of her spine. Hours fall past until the sky begins to brighten, piece by piece the room reassembling from darkness. Frances murmurs something when I go to pull her closer to me, her bottom pressed into my groin. Her fingers flutter where they rest upon a pillow, but she does not wake.

I wonder now about the coming summer months, if this thing between us will be allowed to grow and change, to spread through our lives and not exist only in this bed, between these sheets, in the moving of skin against skin. So elliptical is her life to me that when I look at her now it seems impossible that I could ever have any claim on her. Those eyes, which in sleep flicker beneath their lids, seem destined in waking to look upon another, and still she stirs something possessive in me, as if in knowing that I will never have her I want her all the more.

I get up from the bed and wander into the living room, where the wine bottle stands half empty on a side-table, the whole room reflected in its curve. I can feel the grain of the boards beneath my feet and I think of Da bent over a hammer, sinking row after row of nail heads to exactly the same depth, weighing the hammer in his hand to judge the force that is required.

'Michael?'

When I look back into the bedroom, Frances has lifted herself up on her elbows. She is peering through the murk, wondering what I am doing.

'A glass of water,' I say, and she lowers herself to the pillow again, her eyes on the ceiling.

I stand in the frame of the door and watch her blink a couple of times before sleep claims her and her eyes close again. The first lance of sunlight finds its way into the living room and widens along the wall above the fireplace, finding the mirror that hangs there and the row of clip-framed pictures and keepsakes that are ranged along the mantelpiece.

The fireplace is unused. A bunch of dried flowers tied with string fills the dark gap and from beneath them spill dozens of smooth grey pebbles, carefully arranged so that their quartz seams are aligned.

I pick out a pebble and return to the room where she is still sleeping, arms and legs tangled in the sheets, her lips a little parted. Outside, the street is empty. Sunlight is caught in the uppermost leaves of the trees. The sky beyond them is blue. When I put the pebble on the windowsill it rocks gently to and fro. She hardly moves when I get back into the bed beside her. I look across her shoulder at the brightening window where the pebble sits on the sill, a shadow thrown around it so that it seems to darken, the oval outline of it as perfectly balanced as an egg.

13 Portnew

I remember the eggs, secure in the wooden compart-mented trays that Da had built, the paper slips inscribed with the type of bird that had laid them and the date and place that they had been found or stolen, the glass cover that protected them and which Da would fix into place once all the compartments had been filled.

I don't remember exactly when I started to collect the eggs, but I remember why. Two years before Seamus was killed, Conor Hanlon had brought a tray of eggs into school. They had been his grandfather's and had been found when his parents were clearing out his house after he died, the worm-eaten tray set to one side, where Conor had claimed it, bringing it to school, where it took pride of place on the nature table along-side the pine cones and sycamore seeds, the chestnuts and acorns, the jar of tadpoles. I examined that tray every day until school broke up for summer, crouching to peer more closely at the brown speckled domes, the cobalt dusting on those delicate white curves, looking for the almost imperceptible shake that would tell me that, miraculously, there was something alive in there.

While Da built the trays and compartments to hold the eggs, I set about collecting them from the low cliffs that stumbled away from the western edge of the town, where birds circled endlessly day after day and the rock faces were streaked with white. From where the beach ran out to rock I watched their comings and goings for hours on end. I could pinpoint a gannet's nest beyond the hundreds of gulls' nests, and then, at the highest point of the cliffs, a pair of ospreys guarded a narrow cleft beneath a steep overhang, the prize of an osprey egg almost too wonderful to imagine.

I spent much of that summer collecting and cataloguing the eggs, not only from the sea cliffs but from the edge of a saltwater marsh on the other side of town, where a collapsed railway embankment had closed a brook's route to the sea, and from the quarry, where kites and sparrowhawks built their nests.

It was the chance discoveries that made the summer. A chough's nest stumbled upon in a clutch of heather along the cliff top, the hen scuttling away beneath the wiry blossoms, and I rushing home with an egg in each trouser pocket, warm and alive with potential. Another time I noticed a wading bird dragging a crisp bag backwards along the beach after the visitors had left for the day. I followed its trail and discovered the eggs sitting on a bed of litter and ice-cream sticks at the foot of a dune, the red tag of the wader's tongue darting back and forth in pitiful threat as it implored me to leave. The eggs were tiny and almost translucent, and when I held them against the light I could see, X-ray like, the grey shape of a wing tucked against the inside of each shell. I set them side by side in the cabinet, like brother and sister.

My interest waned after that summer had ended and, with Conor gone, I felt alone in my pursuit.

But it was to the eggs that I strangely returned in the weeks after Seamus had been killed, dragging the cabinets from beneath the bed and asking Da to fix them to the wall once Catherine had moved back into her own room.

'What do you want to be doing that for?' Da asked when I pointed out where I wanted the fixing brackets to go.

I shrugged, but Da put the cabinets up anyway, mapping their place on the wall with a tape measure and spirit level. The cards had yellowed during the years that they had languished in the dark, the black Indian ink bleeding yellow into the paper. At night I could just make out the pale and perfect forms of the eggs, secure in their compartments, the memory of their collection and cataloguing returning me to the days when Seamus was still a presence in our lives, before Ma shrank from us, and before Da gave up working with wood.

I had discovered a pair of shiny new padlocks swinging on the workshop door when we returned from Seamus's funeral. They gleamed in the band of sun which had divided the yard and through which the hens had rushed through to reach the corn that Ma had scattered on the cobbles for the first time in three days.

I had waded through the scrum of feathers to examine the padlocks. Never before had I seen the workshop locked, even though the yard was open to the street through the arch at the side of the house. Da had been trusting enough of people to leave it open, and with himself and Seamus coming and going all day long it was rarely empty for longer than a couple of hours. I had pulled at the padlocks but they were fast, the words UNION and HARDENED inscribed on their heavily ribbed sides, the shanks as thick as my little finger.

I didn't get the chance to ask Da why the workshop was locked, but I soon had my answer.

Da pedalled the bicycle into the yard and the squealing of the brakes sent the hens flying in all directions.

Catherine and I rushed to the door.

The bicycle was black and heavily framed, the chain

enclosed in a metal case, the brakes operated by metal rods. Rust climbed up the mudguards, bubbling beneath the paintwork and smothering the nuts and bolts that secured the guards to the frame. The chrome-work on the spokes had long since vanished, and the cloth loops on the hubs had failed to keep them free of oil and dust. But it had a new leather saddle, still smelling strongly of the tannery, the stitches in the centre seam drawn down deep into the hide so that they would not chafe the seat of Da's trousers.

Da was examining a dynamo which was fixed to the front forks, tracing the wires that led to the front and back lights. He grabbed the handlebars, lifted the front wheel and spun it around, peering into the lens of the front light. He smiled and turned to me.

'Stand over there and look at this, son,' he urged.

I watched the weak glow in the bulb rise and fall as he spun the wheel round and round.

'Do you see that? Do you?' He turned the wheel faster, the palm of his hand dancing off the rubber tyre.

'Aye, Da.' I had seen numerous dynamos on the bicycles that other boys brought to school, the pressure of the mechanism against the tyre edges the bane of evening pushes up Donald Lane as they made their way home.

'Isn't it a wonder of physics, son?'

'Aye,' I said dully, as he proceeded to demonstrate

the rear light to Catherine, who was similarly ordered to look into the lens as he spun the wheel.

After the demonstration was over Catherine retreated to the kitchen, where Ma was scrubbing the linoleum with a deck brush and disinfectant, bent on her knees, the brush held in both hands as she dragged it back and forth across the floor. The sharp smell of the disinfectant was with us almost all of the time now, replacing the sweetness of freshly cut timber, as Ma took to scrubbing every surface as often as she could, as if she could wipe away the stain of Seamus's killing.

I remember an evening, some weeks after Da had first brought the bicycle home, when he stood at the door and watched Ma in silence as she moved across the kitchen floor with the deck brush. The pattern in the linoleum, already faded with the traffic of feet and chair legs, was all but worn away with her scrubbing, so that his reflection fell almost perfectly on the floor before her. She stopped scrubbing but did not turn to look at him.

'What?' she breathed.

'You know what,' Da said.

She bent her head but the brush did not move and the sound of her sobbing rose into the room and pushed out into the yard, where Catherine and I were spreading corn for the hens. It was a soft sobbing, like a single note drawn out on a violin, and all the sadder for it.

Da reached over and prised the deck brush from her fingers. He laid his hand gently in the space between her shoulder blades. One after another her tears fell onto the linoleum.

The constant cleaning came to an end after that, but Ma never seemed the same again. It was as though so much of her had retreated from life that what remained was but a shell.

The workshop stayed locked. The shine on the padlocks dulled with time so that by winter the words inscribed on the shanks were sinking beneath a layer of tarnish.

Da took off each morning on his bicycle, a wooden ladder tied to the back carrier and the crossbar with rope, two buckets swinging from the handlebars, rags spilling from the pockets of his jacket. Unable to face the workshop again, he had set himself up as a window cleaner, often cleaning the panes of windows that he had built or repaired over the years, silently remarking upon his own workmanship, the smooth-running sashes and snugly-fitting frames.

Da returned to his little notebook with its lists of names, cycling from one house or business to another, enquiring after work he had done before and offering his services as a window cleaner. With easy humour he deflected those who asked why he had given up on the woodwork.

'Oh, I had a dose of the woodworm myself and wouldn't want to go spreading it about the town,' and, 'My work was so good in the first place that there's nothing gone rotten that needs repair.'

Most did not ask, knowing how the death of a colleague could affect a man, the ending of the simple rituals of work and workplace that carried them through the days and weeks. Seamus's killing still echoed through the town, as though the sound of those three shots would remain forever trapped within the red-bricked streets.

Da went from house to house, mapping the town for custom just as he had once mapped it for carpentry. Sister sent him on to brother, nephew to niece, cousin to cousin. He offered to clean their windows that first time for nothing in the hope of more work later, but tea and biscuits were brought out to him and a couple of pounds folded into his pocket at the end of it anyway. Sometimes he rode the bicycle, unbalanced by the ladder and buckets, but more often he wheeled it along the streets, his sleeves rolled up to his elbows and his jacket folded over the saddle. He stopped whenever he saw us on our way home from school, all his effort put into holding the bicycle steady with one hand while waving with the other, a smile of pride in his work that we did not share.

Sometimes I would see him stretched across a window frame, one foot perched on a narrow window-sill, the other outstretched for balance as he swept the wiper blade across the glass, pushing a film of water before it. It didn't seem him at all; he whom I had so often watched bend lovingly over a length of cherry or beech, fingers sounding the shape and measure of it. There were times when I wanted to peel him away from his reflection in the glass and lead him home to the workshop, turning the padlock keys and reopening the world of wood which, in grief, he had turned his back upon.

Catherine's arms stretched across the blanket of leaves on the railway embankment, white as fallen branches bleached by the sun, her fingers teasing the tiny links of a necklace she had found somewhere along the Ways. Most of the diamanté stones in the cross that hung from the necklace were missing and the metalwork was bent, but to Catherine it was priceless. Plastic bangles rattled on her wrists and she moved them around and along her arm for something to do while we waited for the first train of the holiday season.

The damp of the darker seasons still slept beneath the soil but there was new growth everywhere around us, lime heads of bindweed nosing for a host to fasten its promise of white trumpets to, brambles sifting through the litter of leaves, a startled thrush dancing away from us.

We waited in the leaf-filtered shadow of the rhododendrons for the train, which was late, its slow progress marked by the frequent trips the stationmaster made to the edge of platform, leaning out over the rails to peer down the track.

A feeling of desolation descended as I watched the platform empty. Around us the rhododendrons shuffled their leaves, gulls circled overhead, the tips of their wings flashing like mica, the trail of a jet dissolving in the blue sky. It had always been like this but something was different now, the experience seemed drained and lifeless. We had come here too often to witness the same scene repeated year after year, and in the space of ten or eleven months we had grown older, much older.

Catherine's face lay on her hands, her eyes closed, the long lashes black as spiders' legs. The cleft in her lip had closed over so that it was almost invisible. There were freckles on her nose, an inch of grass trapped in her hair. I took out the magnifying glass that Ma had given me the year before, a fat, clear lozenge fixed in a tortoiseshell rim that folded into a leather cover upon which was embossed PRAY FOR US. While Catherine dozed, I chased creatures across the ground with a narrow beam of hot sun thrown by the glass: woodlice, earwigs, a black beetle which immediately turned over, its thorax cracking with heat until its legs folded and unfolded no more. I turned a pile of dry leaves to ash, watching the sweet grey smoke drift upwards.

'Hey!' Catherine woke with a start. The beam had caught her elbow.

'Sorry!' I flipped the magnifying glass back into its cover.

'Wee child!' she scorned, turning over on her back, hair spilling across her face, skirt riding up her legs. Her fingers sought a loop of the necklace which lay pooled in the hollow between her neck and breastbone. She pressed it between her lips, the pink tip of her tongue flinching at the sour metal taste, but still she left it there, kinked into the cleft.

Her white T-shirt had been bought two summers before and did nothing to disguise her new breasts, their twin shadows lying beneath thin cotton. I watched her eyes moving behind their lids, her forehead smooth as eggshells, skin as pale as linen. Catherine had changed.

It wasn't the last day we spent on the railway embankment together, but it was the last I can clearly remember. I desperately wanted it to continue as it had before, innocent and unalloyed, yet as each small hour led to another, like the links in the necklace Catherine had found, they gathered towards something blemished and cheap.

*

'Go away you now, Michael.' There was a sharpness in Catherine's voice as she stood there, hands on her hips, her head tipped slightly forward. 'Go on.'

I said nothing but waited for her to turn around and continue down the street. She straightened her skirt and turned, new shoes clicking on the pavement, moving between the shadows of trees. I followed her at a distance but I could tell by her pace and the stiffness of her gait that she knew I was still there.

There was little else to do but follow Catherine. Niall O'Keefe and Joe Lowry, my two best school-friends, had been packed off to relatives in Derry for the summer. Their mothers both worked as seam-stresses in a nearby town and Niall and Joe spent every school holiday in Derry. Upon their return they would tell me about the army patrols there, the upturned and burned-out cars, the running and shouting in the streets at night, the drumming of RUC batons on shields as they advanced, and the deep silence if there was rain.

We re-created the riots in the Ways: Niall and I creeping forward beneath dustbin lids, with sticks for batons, while Joe threw stones at us. We changed places now and again, but it was always best to be an officer, the sharp rattle of the stones on the lid just an inch from your head, knuckles whitening on the fat stick until you could see Niall's or Joe's feet and then you would swing the stick at their ankles and the game was over. Once, unknown to Niall and I, Joe had found a milk bottle which he filled with water and launched amidst the stones with a sudden cry of 'petrol bomb!' It clattered off Niall's shield and burst at my feet, spattering us with water and glass. When I looked up I saw Mr Bingham advancing behind Joe, his face as black as thunder, arm outstretched for Joe's collar. At the last moment Joe noticed Bingham's shadow looming next to his own and feinted to one side before vaulting the wall as Niall and I turned for a gap between two houses that would take us onto Wickham Lane, the metal clatter of the abandoned dustbin lids ringing in the air after us.

Catherine had taken to wandering down to the promenade and the strand, drifting along in the crowds of visitors, sometimes venturing to the water's edge, where she removed her runners and paddled up to her ankles along the tide line. After a while she would return to the sea wall to sit and eat ice cream, her eyes scanning the bodies stretched out on the beach in front of her: women shuffling their clothes off beneath huge striped towels; men leaning back on their elbows, beer cans balanced on their stomachs; a thin woman in the barest of bikinis, ribs like piano keys, her tanned skin glistening with oil, the whiteness of the soles of her feet; naked toddlers wobbling from windbreaks to the sea and back again, cries like those of the seagulls soaring overhead.

Catherine's pink tongue gathered the white ice

cream, her eyes steadily watching the backs of the young men whose arms were blue with tattoos, their necks and shoulders burning under the sun. She swung her legs like a girl of half her age but she dreamed of the young men, the otherness of them that had come from the city to our town. For most of that summer she went there to sit and watch, her bared-birch skin untouched by the sun, stippled with goose pimples on the cooler days when the visitors were few and the sea turned the colour of mortar. Sometimes, schoolfriends joined her, sitting along the sea wall like starlings on a telegraph wire, pointing to some of the boys on the beach, hands snapping back across their mouths to stifle a laugh whenever a face smiled back in answer to an extended finger. But mostly Catherine sat alone, ignoring the stares of those who noticed the blemish of her lip, the change in their stride when they slowed for a better look, the whispers.

I watched her from the shadows of a timbered shelter where a man came each day to scour the *Racing Post* for form, a spaniel at his feet, the leash limply looped on the concrete.

Once I watched a boy of about her own age approach to ask her name, his strong city accent carrying to where I sat. Catherine didn't answer, her legs swung, a seam of ice cream between her lips. The boy stood there for a long while looking at her, thickly freckled, his hair newly cropped so that there was a crescent-shaped rash across the nape of his neck, immune to her silence and the jeers of his friends.

'You must be a Taig after all,' he said in exasperation when eventually he turned away, dragging his feet across the sand. But her legs swung on regardless, and she turned her face a little so that she could better reach a trickle of ice cream which had run along her wrist.

14 London

'Something has got to give,' Frances says. 'This heat is too much.' She is standing at the window, wrapped in a towel. Her wet hair is gathered into another white towel, which is stacked on her head like an ice-cream cone. There are beads of water across her shoulders that begin to slide away when she moves. When I lay my hand against her neck, she draws her shoulders together like the wings of a bird that is ready to take flight.

'Aye,' I say. 'It's fierce hot the day.'

She reaches to take my hand when I go to stand a little closer to her, pressing against the towel, which is damp with water and thick with the smell of her.

'Frances,' I whisper, but she does not appear to hear me.

With a surprising firmness she lifts my hand from

her neck and removes it to my side. There is barely an inch between us but suddenly it feels like a mile.

For a moment the memory of the passion of our lovemaking comes back to me like a grip in my chest, the panting of her breath, how she held my gaze in hers and how her fingers stitched themselves into my hair, the way she surrendered herself so completely to it. The hours that have passed between then and now might be centuries.

She turns away from the window and the street that is already sweating, the trees leaking sap, ripples of heat rising from the roofs of cars, a dog lying in the narrow shade of a gatepost. Her wet footprints on the wooden floor stretch away from me towards the bedroom door.

When I push open the door she is standing in front of the mirror, the towel dropped to the floor. She is achingly beautiful. I can still feel her in my hands, like the smoothest elastic clay. The sweet taste of her lingers in my mouth.

'Michael, don't,' she says when she sees me.

She crouches down to retrieve the towel and covers herself with it. Her head is bowed. When I back out of the bedroom, she clicks the door shut so that I cannot see her dressing herself.

My fists grip and ungrip so that my nails sink into my palms. Frances does not want me, so what am I doing here? I can feel anger rumbling somewhere deep and dark inside me. I want to walk out of her door and slam it shut behind me, slam it shut on these last few months with Frances. Out on the street I am no one, out on the street I can begin all over again.

The living room has fallen curiously dark, like a shadow thrown across things when you know they should be bright. In the sky that is visible above the houses opposite, a thunderhead cloud is filling and rising. A breeze stirs the street below, pulling some of the leaves from the trees. The air is boiling.

There is no warmth in these spare rooms now. They seem as cold and hard as the stones arranged in the fireplace. The blank walls say nothing, like the walls of a cell.

When she comes out of the bedroom I feel my heart rising in my chest. I don't know what I fear. She is dressed. Her head is still bowed, her hair sticking together in thick damp strands. Her feet are bare. While she looks around the room for something she puts the back of her hand to her nose and sniffles a little. It is easy to see that she has been crying, but I don't know what to say to her now.

When she finds her shoes she sits on the edge of the sofa to put them on. 'It's going to rain,' she says.

'Aye.'

She mutters something that I don't hear and bends again to slip her heels into her shoes.

'I think we could go out for coffee,' she brightens, standing up. 'Before the rain.'

We go to a café nearby where the tables are squeezed tightly together apart from one which looks out onto the street. The steel tables have mosaic tiles set into them and the chairs are mismatched. Faded theatre posters line the walls and the stars that have been painted into the dark blue ceiling have yellowed with age and cigarette smoke. Frances orders coffee and croissants from the counter at the back. We stare out of the window for a while at the people hurrying across the darkening street. The wind blows over the board outside the café and a waiter goes to bring it in. People's clothes stick to them and flutter about their limbs. Litter scurries along the pavement.

'I'm sorry, really sorry,' Frances says after the waitress has brought our coffee and croissants. She doesn't regret going to bed with me but it has confused her. She has never before slept with someone she didn't love at the time.

'You didn't sleep with your husband after you realized your marriage was over?'

'Of course I did!' she exclaims. 'We were married – we shared the same house, the same bed.' She looks hurt and puts her hand across the bottom of her throat in defence. Her voice lowers. 'We made love constantly in those last few weeks, like in the first months after we met, desperately trying to save ourselves with it. It didn't work, of course.'

'You're still in love with him, then?'

She sits there with her head bowed, picking flakes of croissant from her plate and sipping coffee.

'When I think about it,' she says eventually, 'I feel we lost each other somewhere along the way, and ever since then we've been trying to find the people we married.'

I can only think of other people who have been lost to me too, and the years I have wasted looking for them in other people. Now it seems that another is about to go.

Frances looks out at the street, where everything is changing to the colour of slate. The grey light falls on her face, which looks older now, her eyes red-rimmed, her hair dulled.

We say nothing for a while. Customers come and go, folding and unfolding newspapers, greeting the waiters and waitresses they know with a smile. They talk about the heat of the last few weeks and wonder when the storm will come.

This heat is like the heat of a summer day years ago when I had fallen asleep on the railway embankment in Portnew one afternoon. What I discovered when I woke changed everything for me. I remember fleeing through rhododendrons, the undersides of the leaves as pale as the skin I had just seen revealed. Then, too, the heat had broken into a storm, and afterwards every-thing had been different.

'What did *you* see in me?' Frances asks without warning, as if she has never considered it before.

'You were beautiful and different,' I say. 'Your hair, your face, the whiteness of your skin. You looked perfect and you seemed so proud of yourself. I thought you didn't need anyone else in the world, and I was drawn to that.'

'But I need other people more than anything else,' she says. 'Couldn't you see?'

'I can now.'

The café's window box is untended and thick with dandelions that are going to seed. As the wind gathers and shakes them I watch the dandelion clocks slowly unwind, each seed spinning out like a tiny shuttlecock, tugged ever upwards until they are lost from sight.

The dandelion clock reminds me of Catherine, the stem held between her fingers and her mouth forming a crooked 'O' as she sent the seeds sailing out across the railway embankment. She would look at them go with a great sadness, as if she had released them through the bars of a cell, imagining their flight into a world we did not then know and which was filled with possibilities.

A gust snaps at the window box and every stem is suddenly bare.

'I have to go,' Frances says. Her coffee has grown cold, a croissant lies half eaten on her plate.

'Aye.'

She stands up and turns around. The café windows rattle and the first fat spatters of rain are falling, scratching at the glass, staining the pavements. Frances gives me the weakest of smiles and offers me her hand, which I take and squeeze. The bones feel hard and angular, stiff with tension. She wants to go.

I watch her cross the street, the wind pulling at her clothes and hair, rain drawing patterns on her skirt. She never looks back. I watch her for as long as I can, until a bread van pulls up outside the café and I can see her no more.

15 Portnew

It was Fiona Marshall who told me what I had not wanted to hear.

'Catherine has a fella, did you not know?'

I had gone to Fiona's father's bookmaker's shop to place a bet for Da. It was Fiona's job to climb onto the counter and walk along it to change the odds chalked up on the blackboard that hung above it. A veil of dust fell about her legs as she wiped and wrote, coating the heavy black shoes she wore. As she worked her way along the counter she would pull the hem of her skirt close to her so that the men who came to place a bet or collect winnings wouldn't be able to steal an upward glance.

The men stood with their backs to the room, examining the racing pages pinned to the walls, caps tilted up off their foreheads as they scanned the lists down and across. They changed places as they completed each page, marking form on the cardboard backs of the pads of betting slips that Marshall handed out to all his regulars.

'Yes, Michael?' Fiona said, stepping down from the counter and brushing chalk dust from her front.

'It's a bet for the Da I'm after,' I blurted.

'Aye.'

Fiona was the plainest of girls. Her mousy brown hair was serviceably tied back into a ponytail, the puppy fat of childhood clinging on for so long now that it looked as if it would never leave, muddying her features and crowding the small brown eyes and snub nose. I liked her because she seemed within reach in a way that the prettier girls weren't.

'Give me a wee minute, Michael, will you?' she said, and I nodded.

While I waited for her to take the other men's bets I flicked through a stack of newspapers at the end of the counter, page after page of news and photographs of the living, the injured, the missing and the dead, each face just one among dozens, then hundreds, then thousands, each individual shadow merging with the rest as their collective darkness descended upon us with the passing of years.

When Fiona was free I placed my bet, carefully writing the details of the meeting, race and horse onto the slip before pushing it across the counter to her. 'Each way, please,' I said, handing her the money.

As I waited for the race to come on the radio I noticed the pattern of the afternoon in the betting shop, the long silence before the almost reluctant shuffle of feet towards the counter, and then the grunts of encouragement that greeted the entering of the final furlongs on the television, climbing to the cursing and whooping of loss and victory before the shop again returned to silence. I now knew why men allowed it to become the rhythm of their days in the absence of work or other things: the small sparks of excitement that were looked forward to with everything any promise holds, fulfilled or broken in a few moments; the thundering of hooves on turf echoed in the beating of their hearts, which would cease if their bet fell or slumped to back-marking, the now useless pink slips drifting like leaves to the floor.

Da's horse came in second. There'd be two pounds to take home to him. Fiona gave them to me even before I had a chance to hand over the slip. It was the last race of the day and when I turned around the shop was empty.

I walked with Fiona through the tawny light of dusk, the streets filled with the sour low-tide smell that I never got used to. She told me that she hated the job in the bookmaker's shop, not because of the work itself but because she felt she owed it to her father to help keep it going while he drank himself to death in the seafront bars.

'Maybe he'll be back to rights soon, Fiona, and then you can get away,' I offered.

'Some hope! You know, your own father and poor uncle have spent enough money in the shop down the years. Their wee bets were nothing, mind, to the bets some would put on a horse that hadn't a hope in hell of even making it to the winning post.'

It was then that she told me that Catherine had a boyfriend.

'What?' I said, not certain that I had heard her right.

'Raymond. Raymond Harvey, your sister's fella.'

'Catch yourself on!' I said. 'Catherine doesn't have a fella.'

We stopped at the kerb to wait for a car to pass before crossing, its headlights sweeping the walls as it turned, the beam illuminating the litter and leaves gathered along one side of the Ways. I struggled to take in what I had heard: that my own sister had betrayed and abandoned me.

Fiona crossed the street and set off along the Ways without hesitating.

'His family have a newsagent's shop out there on the Antrim road,' Fiona said when I had caught up with her. 'You know the one next to the garage?'

'Aye.' I didn't know it, but that didn't matter now.

'They've been stepping out for weeks. Everyone knows.'

All along the Ways I tried to assemble the evidence I had missed, the time she must have stolen to be with him. There was nothing I could put my finger on – she had slipped away from me and I could hear her laughing.

'Are you sure?' I asked.

'Of course I'm sure.' Fiona smiled, seeing the confusion on my face.

'Do you know him yourself, then?'

'I do, sort of. He's a Prod, you know.'

A Protestant. In my surprise I hadn't stopped to wonder at his name.

'Have you never seen him waiting for her at the school gates? He sure takes some stick from our own lads. It must be love that keeps him there, and your sister leaves the poor fellow waiting just long enough for everyone to see.'

I tried to remember if I had noticed anyone outside the gates, but I couldn't. I imagined a stocky, narrow-faced boy, his hair cropped short, thin lips drawn wide into a smile, anger on his brow. 'No,' I said.

'Will you set the table for me?' Ma said, folding a magazine away behind the bread bin.

It was a release to remove my school books to the front room, where I might work on them later, the imagined picture of Catherine and Raymond Harvey that dogged every waking moment blurred now with the ritual of the setting of places, the careful symmetry of knives and forks on either side of the place mats with their laminated portraits of ducks.

It seemed impossible to concentrate on anything until I could be certain that what I had heard was true, that Catherine was seeing Raymond Harvey, a Protestant boy from across the town. All day in school I had imagined them together, walking along the promenade, winding their way hand in hand through the amusements, where only a few desperate gamblers now lingered, or strolling along the Ways, where they would stop to kiss in the safety of the shadows and his hand would slip beneath her school jumper.

After school I had crossed the road and hidden in a doorway to watch for Raymond, but when Catherine emerged she was with the friends she usually walked home with.

'Where's Catherine the night?' Da asked, coming through the back door and sweeping a draught of cold in upon us. He washed his hands at the sink, clapping them between the towel to get the blood back into his fingers.

'She's out at Paula Garvey's house,' Ma answered.

'They're doing a school project together and she'll eat there.'

'I haven't seen her for days.' Da sat into the table

next to Ma, picked up his knife and fork and began to eat as soon as the plate had been set in front of him, any chance of conversation now closed until the meal had been taken.

Da and Ma ate and slept together but were beginning to move in separate orbits. Now there was nothing to be heard from downstairs as I lay in bed each evening, Ma sitting in the kitchen with her tea and magazines while Da occupied the armchair next to the radiogram in the front room. Sometimes he would fall asleep in the armchair and Ma would switch off the light before ascending the stairs, leaving him alone there in the glow of the tuning dial and the flickering firelight bulb in the hearth. The last night-time conversation that once had raked over the coals of the day had now fallen to embers as they sought to avoid that which troubled them most.

'She'll be safe coming back through the Terraces?' Da asked.

'Aye, she will,' Ma said. 'Paula's brother will walk her home once he gets in from his shift at the cement plant.'

There had been trouble in the ladder of streets that began at Simmons Street and ran down to the seafront, every gable of which now housed a Loyalist mural of one sort or another. What Catholics had once lived there had moved on, squeezing in with relatives or going to other towns and villages altogether, Protestant families from the smaller cottages above the railway embankment taking their place. On certain nights there were self-proclaimed security checks at every entrance to the Terraces from Donald Lane.

'I'm away out,' I announced once the meal was finished.

I closed the door on them and went out into the darkened streets, where the smoke of numerous chimneys had settled and each curtained window threw its shape of dull light upon the night. Every sound could be heard: the chatter of televisions in the front rooms, the rumble of a few cars in neighbouring streets, the opening and closing of front doors as men made their way to the bars for the evening.

Da and Seamus had once been counted among their number, but after Seamus had been killed the knock on the door had seldom come for Da, fear of saying the wrong thing putting the men off calling in the first weeks of mourning that had stretched to months and now years. Perhaps Da welcomed it, not wanting to sit at that same spot at the bar where he and Seamus had always sat, examining the counter-top for wear and tear in the years since they had first installed it, remarking on how the grain had dulled with the action of spilled stout and the scrubbing of innumerable cloths.

Before reaching the Orange Hall I cut along the Ways so that I could get up the hill to the end of

Bickerstaffe Street and watch out for anyone turning down Welwyn Road.

As I waited, the night seemed the death of that summer and all summers before, seagulls floating greyly overhead, a cloak of smoke and mist hanging above the town. A dull pool of light at the end of the harbour wall illuminated the inscription painted beside the life-ring station: FUCK THE POPE.

I grew cold waiting. There were flecks of rain in the air now and a breeze had begun to shift the fug from between the houses. I watched the rain filter down through the lamplight like falling stars and felt it prickle upon my cheeks. I imagined the spots of rain falling on Paula's brother's donkey-jacket, a Dalmatian pattern amidst the grey dust of the cement plant.

Their voices came to me through the rain-flecked stillness long before I saw them coming down Bicker-staffe Street. I knew from the way they were talking that it wasn't Paula's brother at all, the intimate edges of whispers that carry no matter how small you make your voice. I stepped back into the shadows and watched their silhouettes move into the light, Cather-ine's hand gripped firmly in Raymond's, her head slightly tilted towards his shoulder.

They turned down Welwyn Road, Catherine swinging on Raymond's arm to lean out over the kerb. He loosened his grip for a moment and she began to fall, but he caught her almost before she noticed. Her laugh rang out between the houses. 'Do that once more, Raymond Harvey, and I might have to kiss you!' she squealed, whereupon he let go again before pulling her back against him and burying his face in her hair. She was shuddering with a laughter that rippled right along her spine. She stretched an arm across his back and fixed her thumb under his trouser belt.

He was tall and thin, his skin sallow, his hair black. There was warmth in his face and he moved with a relaxed ease.

When they turned into the Ways I left my lookout post and crossed the road to follow them at a distance. I could see the prints of their shoes in the fresh rain on the pavement, the rough grid of his working soles alongside the finer print of her pumps. I stuck my head around the entrance to the Ways to make sure that the path was clear but there was nothing to be seen. I could still hear Catherine's laugh funnelling its way back between the walls, broken by the deeper tones of Raymond's voice. I ventured out into the middle of the path where a puddle had formed and turned to quicksilver under the light of stars and lamps, yet still the path ahead of me was empty and still their voices carried, seeming even closer now.

I returned to the shadows and padded along the path, their voices bouncing on ahead of me. As I came to the point where the Ways opened out onto the end of our street, their voices began to fade and then were completely lost. The path seemed suddenly desolate. I could hear the rustle of litter trapped in corners and the slamming of doors as children were sent out with buckets to the coal scuttles in the back yards, but nothing else. When I ran out onto our street it was empty, a streetlight buzzing as a fuse began to fail.

Everything was still and waiting. It was as if Catherine and Raymond had been spirited away.

Christmas came. Our street, which on the darkest nights had been lit up by the light thrown from the Christmas trees set behind every bared window, was darker than I could ever remember as people drew their curtains for fear that having a tree on open display might make them a target for the Loyalist gangs who sometimes crossed Donald Lane to break windows with golf clubs and bats. The houses at the end of our street had it worst, their brickwork often daubed with paint, Glennon's front window criss-crossed with masking tape as if there was a war on. Megan Keane woke one morning to find the head of a golf club embedded in her front door. Once or twice the RUC parked a Land Rover at the bottom of the street but still the gangs attacked, the officers directing their powerful lamps into the faces of those of us who dared to lean from upstairs windows to see what was happening on the street below.

A few days after Christmas I cycled out along the

Antrim road to see where Raymond's family had their shop. The houses thinned out beyond the town, a scattering of guesthouses overlooking the old harbour and the Viceroy Hotel, which was now a retirement home, the lawn riddled with dandelions, a pair of empty wheelchairs visible behind the wired safety glass of the patio doors. In primary school we had been brought there by bus every Christmas Eve to sing carols for the residents, our unbroken voices sailing through the brown and cream corridors, ignored by the residents, who barely stirred in their beds and armchairs, apart from one tall and rangy man who squeaked his Zimmer frame right up in front of us and stared as we sang, eyeballing each one of us and smiling wickedly, leaning his elbows on the frame to clap slowly after every carol.

Raymond's family's shop sat in the shadows of the canopy of a new BP petrol station. The shop front had been freshly painted to escape the gloom cast by its neighbour, and the plain sign above the window simply read HARVEY in red wooden letters. A *Belfast News-letter* board stood on the broken tarmac outside, the only indicator of the family's allegiances. I watched a Ford Granada draw up at the filling station and while the father filled the tank a gaggle of children clambered from the back seat and bundled into Harvey's, the girls in velvet dresses with their hair tied in pigtails, the boys in shirts and ties with matching sleeveless pullovers. It was visiting day, the children desperate to spend the small change collected from relatives. They re-emerged as I pedalled off, the boys clutching comics, the girls plastic tubes of brightly coloured sweets.

As I cycled home I thought of Da and Ma and what they didn't know about Catherine and Raymond – which was everything. This was a secret I had to keep between me and Catherine because I knew that the truth of it would hurt them more than I or they could bear. Catherine did not yet know that I knew, and she would only tell me once whisper upon whisper had begun to reach Da's or Ma's ear, collecting there like the weight of water against a dam wall. By sharing it with me she could release some of the pressure. I could cover for her, deny all knowledge, tell them that everything was the same at school.

But no matter what happened, I could never tell them the truth. I loved them too much to tell them that Catherine was in love with a Protestant boy from across the town, when it was Protestants who had killed Seamus, Ma's brother, Da's best friend, and torn such a hole in our lives that it had not yet begun to heal.

Portnew quickly shook that winter off, the amusements owners heralding the arrival of better weather by applying fresh coats of bright paint to the arcades, ladders carried back and forth as blown bulbs were replaced and neon signs checked.

Da and I had stopped for lunch at the head of a row of steps which led down to the promenade. We ate corned-beef sandwiches and drank tea from a flask and a Tupperware box carried in a bucket hanging from the handlebars of Da's bicycle.

'Do you know something, son?' Da started, pushing a ball of bread and meat to the side of his mouth as he went to speak. 'There's regular customers of mine who've begun to wash their own windows. All of a sudden, mind.'

We had been busy all morning going from one house to another and I was already tired from filling and refilling the buckets with fresh water and holding the ladders steady while staring at the soles of Da's shoes. I looked at him sceptically.

'True as I'm standing here, son,' he defended. 'We're run ragged the day, but come Monday there'll be nothing doing. Nothing at all.'

Spring was the busiest time for Da as people took to tidying their yards and gardens and the sunlight striking the windows showed up the grey scum that had gathered over winter. We had hardly seen him during the fortnight before Easter the previous year, so busy had he been with the guesthouse and hotel owners and shopkeepers who wanted their windows crystal clean in advance of the arrival of the first visitors.

He unscrewed the flask and poured tea into the cap,

which doubled as a cup. 'I wouldn't mind but they're our own kind as well,' he added.

Now I realized why. The whisper that Catherine was seeing Raymond Harvey had spread beyond the walls of our school and into the streets, working its way from terrace to terrace and house to house. I imagined the mothers clearing buckets and retrieving cobwebbed ladders from dusty attics, desperate to get their windows clean before Da appeared at the door-step so that they wouldn't have to face him. How could they know that he was ignorant of it all, that their panes of clean, wet glass were a complete mystery to him?

Da stood perfectly still beside his bike, chewing on another sandwich, one hand laid on a fat black hand-grip, gazing at the promenade below and wondering at the customers who had taken to washing their own windows. Beyond him, far beyond the promenade and the ribbed expanse of grey sand, the tide paused at full ebb, the faintest trace of a white edge upon the horizon. Clouds moved across the stretch of sea and sand like drifting continents, pushed out by an offshore breeze to the tide line where they waited, brooding.

I sometimes followed Catherine and Raymond along the Ways or down to the old harbour. They were careful not to hold hands in case they met someone they knew, but sometimes they kissed, quick as sparrows, so that you'd hardly know they'd touched at all.

While they ate ice cream or Coke floats and strolled along the promenade, I took to wandering the shore, kicking at the flotsam brought in on the last tide and whatever the waves had unburied.

I collected the finest of these things in my pockets, pebbles, bottles and porcelain. The empty display boxes from my egg-collecting days were opened again and I would spend hours rearranging what I had found, the bottles and pebbles by size and colour, the porcelain fragments by pattern alone, in an attempt to make them fit together.

Our lives were moving so inexorably apart, Ma from Da, and Catherine from the rest of us, like continental drift. In some small way my collecting of the fragments on the beach was an attempt to make sense of things, to put things back together and make them whole again.

The first ripples of disapproval that Da had felt in that week before Easter had become a tide by the end of May. He spent most afternoons at home now, listening to the radio, listlessly drifting from front room to kitchen. He revisited his book of names and addresses again and again as he looked for new business, his thumb pressed upon a name as he sought out some connection or other. Most of the names in the book had pencil lines struck through them. Every so often he would get up and tuck the book back into his jacket pocket, fasten his trousers with bicycle clips, rinse the sponges and take off across town, buckets clattering against the front forks. I watched him sail past as I returned from school, one arm raised in salute, a grim set to his face.

At night, as I examined the display cases on my bedroom wall, I could hear them counting the money, the few coins that were left divided among them and dropped into their pockets. Ma stored the rest in Russian dolls that stood on a shelf above the cooker, each doll holding a separate sum for food or electricity or gas.

There were often arguments about the money, Ma wanting every penny kept back until the housekeeping and bills were paid.

'I need to have a pint or two to keep me sane!' Da would protest. 'The lads in the bar always pass on word of any work that's going. If I don't show my face there once in a while they'll think I'm not looking for it. Catch yourself on, pet!'

I heard the chink-chink of the coins as Da scooped them off the edge of the table and into his hand. He would fold a few notes between his thumb and forefinger before pushing them into his breast pocket.

*

The RUC took Da in when they stopped him on the street and found his book of names. It was a Friday and Ma was waiting at the front door when I got home from school.

'Did you see your sister?' she shouted as I dragged myself down the street towards her.

I shrugged my shoulders, assuming that Catherine had taken off somewhere with Raymond.

'The police have your Da,' she started, ushering me inside and looking around the street before closing the door.

Her eyes were red from crying and there were two mugs of tea gone cold and grey on the kitchen table. A bucket of feed for the hens still stood inside the back door and the sound of the birds' desperate scratching on the cobbles could be heard through the kitchen window. I wondered how she could have borne to sit for so long at the table with the noise of their claws on the stones.

'They stopped him beside the war memorial and searched him on the spot,' Ma said. 'When they found his little book they threw him in the back of the Land Rover and took him to the station.' She dragged a bunched-up tissue from her sleeve and dabbed at her cheeks. 'Sure, your Da's done nothing, and now they say they're keeping him in for the weekend.'

I was looking at her standing against the table, my school bag still hanging from my shoulder. I was trying to listen to what she was saying but all I could hear were the hens in the back yard, their scratching growing louder and louder as Ma's face blurred and the room began to dissolve around me.

'Now, now.' Ma bent over me, folding onto her knees, a hand pressing into the small of my back. 'There's no need to cry, Michael. Your Da's done nothing wrong. Sure, he'll be back to us in no time.' She clutched me to her, a smell of perfume and Jif in her clothes, and beyond that the smell of her skin that took me back to the years before I had got too big to be held like this or to want to be held like this.

'Will he be interned like Lorcan Brady was?' I remembered Cormac and Kevin standing in their pyjamas on the night the RUC men came for their father, their faces bright red from crying, limp as dolls. It was months before he was released, during which time they had begun to tell their classmates that their Da was an IRA hero, a sniper, a bomber. He had taken a strap to their legs when he heard what they had been saying.

'No, no, of course he won't,' Ma said, hugging me all the harder. The tears were running again on her cheeks and I wanted to tell her then about Catherine and Raymond, but I couldn't, not because I didn't want to betray Catherine but because I knew it would help none of us: not me; not Da, alone in a cell in the station, waiting for the interviewing sergeant; not Ma, kneeling on the hard linoleum floor of the kitchen; and not Catherine, who, ignorant of all this, was walking out with Raymond.

Ma tried to make dinner before going back to the RUC station, but she kept forgetting about the sausages under the grill and the potatoes boiled over again and again so that the kitchen was filled with the smell of burning meat and boiling potatoes by the time Catherine appeared.

'Where have you been all this time?' Ma called out when she heard Catherine letting herself in through the front door.

Her only answer was the thud of feet on the stairs and the creaking of bedsprings when Catherine sat on the edge of her bed to change out of her school clothes.

'Your Da's been taken in by the police,' Ma whispered as she put our dinners down in front of us. The plates clinked together with the shaking in her hands.

'How was I supposed to know?' Catherine protested, but I could see the surprise in her face. 'Why would they take Da in?' she asked. 'Sure, Da's done nothing.'

'They found his book,' I said. 'The one with all the names in it.'

'They don't need an excuse these days,' Ma added.

Catherine didn't ask any more questions or seem to want any explanation. While Ma and I picked through our food, Catherine ate hers quickly, twisting a lock of hair between her fingers. When she had finished she took the bowl of lime jelly that Ma had made the night before and spooned some into her bowl.

'Are you in a hurry someplace?' Ma asked her.

'I just want to go out, Ma. It's a nice evening.'

'Jesus! Catch yourself on, Catherine!' Ma shouted. 'Your Da is in the station and you're talking about the nice evening that's in it!'

Ma never shouted and the kitchen seemed bare and hollow afterwards, the anger of the words just hanging there around us.

'You're coming to the station with Michael and me,' Ma said quietly but firmly. 'It'll look better if the three of us show up, and anyway, I don't want the whole town knowing that your Da's been taken in.'

Catherine sat in Da's chair and wrapped her arms around her knees. She seemed bored by it all but by choosing to sit in his chair I knew that in her heart she was as worried about Da as Ma and I were. Her gaze travelled across the kitchen counter, the postcards pushed in around the power sockets, the fruit bowl with its apple and brown banana, the broken mixer, the tap whose handle Seamus had temporarily replaced with a door hinge screwed down into the spindle and which Ma would not now allow to be properly fixed. In their timeless simplicity I knew that they were a reassurance to Ma, that she would have looked for them as soon as she came back from burying Seamus, or whenever Da returned empty-handed, that even when she lifted her head from the newspaper headlines she would have been happy to see them still there, as if finding them the same she could believe that nothing in her life had changed.

These things meant little to Catherine. She was restless while she waited for Ma to finish, impatiently pursing and unpursing her lips, fidgeting with a tear in the knee of her jeans through which a sliver of that impossibly white skin showed.

When we arrived at the station the officer said that only Ma could go in. We waited beyond the steel and wire cage that enclosed the door. Every so often a shape appeared behind the thick green-glass panel in the middle of the door and I caught the gleam of the badge set into the front of the officer's cap. Catherine went and sat on the garden wall of one of the houses opposite whose windows had been bricked up because they faced the station and were considered a security threat. She was wearing a navy and white striped top that had grown too small for her so that her midriff showed, bellybutton winking whenever she bent forward. The top was stretched into folds across her small chest and the sleeves looked tight upon her arms and shoulders, but it was her favourite thing, worn always with those old jeans and her bare feet pushed into a pair of tan-coloured suede sandals.

She looked so fragile sitting there, willowy limbs

enclosed in her shrunken clothes so that they looked like those of a new-born foal, moving in angles, unable to bear any weight. The breeze which was almost ever-present in Portnew teased and splayed her hair across her forehead and she swept it back with her finger, giving her head the slightest of shakes. When she swung her legs the soles of her sandals scuffed off the pavement and followed some simple rhythm like a melody was playing in her head.

The air had begun to turn that curious shade of blue which descends just before the dusk, laden with dust and the small noises of evening. The streets looked deserted, the sun dully sinking behind their acres of grey slate roofs that slanted towards the sea. It was as if, with the arrival of the Troubles, the RUC station had blighted the area, the shadow of its steel stockades darkening every doorway and yard, the coils of barbed wire invading every view.

When the first stones rattled down the street I barely noticed them, and it wasn't until one rolled almost to my feet that I realized what was happening. I stepped back closer to the station and called out to Catherine:

'Watch out for the stones!'

She lifted her head and gave me one of her withering looks. The rhythm of her swinging legs didn't change once and she never even bothered to look down the street to where a group of boys a little younger than myself were crouched behind a low wall, along which was arranged an armoury of stones and broken bricks. They threw from their crouching position and the stones struck the road and bounced towards us with little force, rattling into the gutter or spinning to a standstill. I watched for the arc of the stones against the indigo sky and it was only when they were confident enough to stand up and throw that I retreated to the other side of the cage that protected the station door. They turned their attention to Catherine then, but she ignored the stones striking the kerb and wall near her, one piece of brick shattering into dust and grit when it caught a gatepost just feet from where she was sitting.

One of the boys broke cover and advanced up the street towards us, wielding a substantial corner of a brick, which he launched towards me before turning quickly on his heel just as it clattered into the steel cage with a terrible racket.

Within seconds the street lit up under a blaze of arc lights from a gantry inside the station, erasing all the shadows and picking out the litter of stones and broken brick on the street.

The boys fled but the drenching light made it impossible for me to see them. Catherine was still sitting on the wall with her hands pressed across her eyes to shield them from the glare, and everything about and around her seemed bleached to nothingness, as if she was caught in a film negative. A moment later the lights went off and she looked up at me, completely without expression, holding my returned gaze for a long time in those strange eyes.

Da was released on Sunday morning. He arrived at the door as we were getting ready for Mass. Ma had me wearing my best clothes: a Confirmation suit which was three years old and at least two sizes too small. The elbow of the brown corduroy jacket had a mildew stain from where it had hung against an outside wall and for all Ma's brushing it was still there, a faint white halo on my sleeve.

Catherine had come downstairs in her jeans and a black sweat shirt with LEVI STRAUSS across the front. Ma was telling her to go back up and put on a skirt or a dress before the jeans rotted off her when the door opened and Da walked in.

'Well?' he said, taking the key out of the lock. 'Aren't you happy to have me home?'

I fell into him and as my arms went around him my sleeve buttons gave way. I felt his hand upon my head, scrubbing my hair. I remember noticing how his jacket still smelled of wood, of willow and poplar, ash and deal, a legacy of the sawdust and shavings that had collected in the seams over the years and which he could never shake off. He leaned over towards Ma and she took his wrist and gripped it so hard that I was afraid she might hurt him, the tendons stretched as if by pulleys. Ma was trying not to cry and the effort of it made her shake so that Da shook too. When I looked up Da was smiling and mouthing something to Ma, his eyes seeming to plead for something from her, like mercy or forgiveness.

Catherine had continued up the stairs, had hardly paused when Da came in, and it was when her bedroom door slammed shut behind her that Ma and I let go of Da.

'Catherine!' Ma called up after her. 'Catherine!'

'Leave her be,' Da said. 'She's upset and doesn't want to show it, the poor wee thing.' He coughed and straightened himself. 'She'll not come down until she's good and ready.'

Ma went into the kitchen, fingers pressed to her temples as if there was an unbearable pressure within the house. We followed her, Da's hand resting on my shoulder. Ma set the kettle to boil and laid strips of fatty bacon on the frying pan. Da sat at the table with his arms spread wide across it in a gesture of innocence.

While the bacon cooked he told us about the two nights he had spent in the station, the same questions asked time and again by different officers.

'At least they never laid a finger on me,' Da added.

Ma put Da's bacon down before him and slumped onto a chair beside me. Da covered her hand with his and squeezed it, folding it like a bird's wing until she looked up at him and smiled feebly. 'I don't know, Jack . . .' she began, but he squeezed her hand again to stop her saying any more.

Da's high humour masked the fear in him, the tremble that was visible in the tines of the fork with which he took the bacon from the plate. He seemed to have grown much, much older in the space of two days, as if the years had suddenly caught up with him.

The front door opened, allowing the noise of a passing car inside before shutting again.

'Has your sister gone out without so much as a by-your-leave?' Ma asked, sitting upright and turning towards the door.

I went out to the hallway and then up the stairs. Catherine's room was empty save for traces of the perfume she wore: sweet and sharp, like sugared limes. Clothes spilled out of a chest of drawers, a bra hung on the back of a chair, a pair of white tennis shoes sat side by side on the bed. A plastic case of Marks & Spencer make-up lay open on the old writing desk beneath the window, a mirror propped up against the windowsill. Catherine had framed the mirror by garlanding its bev-elled edge with red lipstick kisses, the imperfect symmetry of those lips lying there like flightless butter-flies.

I had spent most of a hot July afternoon looking for Catherine when I remembered the railway embank-ment. I hadn't been there for more than a year but I knew that in the cool shade of the rhododendrons there would be some escape from the heat.

A train was waiting on the tracks, the smell of diesel clotting the air around the station, its driver stripped to the waist and slumped in a deckchair on the platform. From Wickham Lane I watched the stationmaster lead his Labrador onto the patch of grass at the end of the platform and then drag the red fire hose off its reel, the spindle creaking through lack of use. When he opened the valve the hose buckled and straightened along the platform before the water sprayed out through the brass nozzle. The stationmaster adjusted the nozzle until eventually the water fanned outwards and down onto the panting dog, which rolled over and over on the grass as the cool water fell.

I scaled the wall and slipped down through the trees where the air seethed with wings: midges, bluebottles, hover flies, a hornet buzzing my ear. Woodlice, beetles and centipedes blundered about at my feet. I crept down into the coolness of the rhododendrons, the dense canopy of their leaves enclosing a sweet musk-like dampness. The rhododendrons were pierced by countless beams of sunlight, as if the sun had been filtered through a colander. The air was fetid and viscous, lying as thickly upon my tongue as a mouthful of oil.

I found the stretch of grass where Catherine and I had spent so many hours, our absence and the heat now allowing the growth of great arcing seed stems that trembled at my footfall. The grass crackled when I sat down to finish the remains of an ice-cream cone I had bought earlier, the wafer sodden and limp and already attracting the attentions of flies. Diaphanous plumes of heat rose all along the railway track, swarming and swerving across the rusted grey colours of the track and its ballast. As I watched the heat rise and the colours separate then coalesce I felt my head tilt forward to rest upon my pulled-up knees, noticing a red tick cross my palm towards the last inch of cone trapped in the angle of my thumb.

Something had changed when I woke up with a start, the brightness scalding my eyes. It was like a single note missed amidst a symphony, a shift in the register of things.

I plucked one of the grass stems from its socket and teased it between my teeth, tasting the sour greenness of its sap. Then something cracked far off to my left where the embankment rose steeply towards the retaining wall at its end, and where the rhododendrons grew to the exclusion of everything else. I stilled the stem between my teeth and rose into a crouch to look around. There was nothing to see but wave after wave of rhododendrons spread beneath the sweeping boughs of the trees, the jewels of their blossoms held aloft. As I was about to sit down again I heard a sudden bustling and a blackbird burst into the air above the embankment, the yellow arrow of its beak just visible against the shadows. I crept along the stretch of grass until I came to the briars, where I stopped again to listen. Nothing.

I crawled back up through the rhododendrons and then over towards the retaining wall, gaining height all of the time so that I could escape across the wall if anything should make a go for me.

It was the familiar navy stripes of Catherine's favourite top that stood out among the chaos of the undergrowth some twenty or thirty feet below me. I inched my way further down the slope, always keeping my eyes on that banner of her top. As I got closer I could see the shape of an arm stretched across the stripes until I was close enough to see them both, Catherine and Raymond sitting side by side on the embankment, the thinnest shaft of sunlight brightening the pool of shadows in which they sat.

I planted my fingers into the mulch to stop myself from sliding and as I carefully sat down I could feel things swarming across the backs of my hands, a multitude of tiny legs and twitching antennae.

They were facing the railway station, which was just visible through the thick mesh of green: grey swatches of stone, iron and wood, the angle of a parapet. Catherine was glancing sideways at Raymond with that veiled, forlorn look I had often seen Ma and Da exchange when I was much younger and before the Seamus thing had happened. That way of looking hypnotized me because I was now old enough to recognize it for what it was: affection, fondness, love and desire. Raymond was talking, the low tones of his voice carrying through the undergrowth. Catherine was nodding ever so gently, her body bending towards his.

I craned my neck to see them better, the myriad leaves and branches shifting back and forth to obscure my view. I froze as I watched them, curious and afraid at the same time, each part of me trembling so much that I feared they might sense it too. I began to feel a little sick and had the sensation of something constantly ascending and descending in my throat.

I crouched on my haunches and carefully inched my way down the slope. My fingers clung to the soil and I could feel rotting leaves against my palms. I could hear some of what they were saying. When I got to a point where I could see them more clearly, Catherine was lying on her back. Her T-shirt was bunched up beneath her shoulders and miniature shafts of sunlight were playing upon her face. I could only see Raymond's back, and their voices dropped to the smallest of whispers.

I wondered why they had come here, remembering the innocent hours Catherine and I had spent at the embankment, her dreams of other places and other people. It seemed a long, long time ago, like a dream that completely disappears upon waking. And now that Catherine was going from me I felt all alone in the world. As I watched Raymond's face drop towards

Catherine's and his hands reach across her body I
turned my eyes away.

The stationmaster's Labrador began barking all of a
sudden, the noise breaking through the undergrowth
like a violent wind. I yelped with fright and momentarily lost my grip in the mulch, my scrabbling feet
sending a shower of dirt and twigs down the slope.
Catherine and Raymond sat bolt upright, her hand
grasping his shoulder for reassurance, but before they
could turn around I was desperately half running and
half crawling my way back towards the line of trees. I
could hear their voices behind me and thought I could
hear my name being called, but everything got tangled
in the rush of branches and leaves as I made my escape.
All the way up the slope I tried to prepare myself for
the clamp of Raymond's hand upon my shoulder, his
hot breath in my ear, but it never came.

When I turned around at Wickham Lane the rhododendrons were still and silent, save for the fury of the
insects that had risen in miasmic clouds above them.

16 London

I have been here before, but never like this. The blunt ache of the loss of love, or the idea of love, vanished like a hole in your life. I have thought of Frances every hour this last week, fragments of her appearing before me like a series of paintings: her mouth, the whorl of an ear, the fold of skin inside her elbow, her shoulder blades angled like boomerangs.

She did not come to school on Monday and a substitute could not be found. A note arrived at the school on Tuesday: she would not be returning for the last week of term. The note did not say why.

On Tuesday evening I went looking for her. An estate agent's board was nailed to the gatepost of her house. My knocks on the door went unanswered. I waited on the steps until it grew dark, but the windows stayed unlit, the curtains half drawn. On Wednesday I telephoned the estate agent and arranged to view her flat that evening. He showed me around the empty rooms, talking urgently, a diary in one fist, Frances's keys dangling from another. The rear windows had been propped open and the flat scoured of even her smell. When I opened the wardrobe a row of wire hangers chimed emptily, the space smelling only of lavender. Just before leaving I noticed the solitary pebble on the bedroom windowsill and slipped it into my pocket, the smoothness of it against my palm a comfort as I made my way home through the streets we had once walked along. I remembered how she had laughed out loud at one point and I paused there to wonder if the echo of it could still be trapped between the highrises. My vision then of a summer of complete happiness was illusory, and whatever had happened between us in her flat that night made everything else we had irretrievable.

Beyond the classroom windows the canal is steeped in the stillness of after-rain, the surface still battened down against the drops that fall heavily from the trees. There is weed in the margins, moss growing among the towpath flagstones, buddleia sprouting from the brickwork of the bridges with their groove-worn curves that are the legacy of the barges, tow ropes and dray horses. An angler sits on a box below the lock, tackle spread in an arc around him, a float tethered to the end of his fishing pole. He is bent over, as if by the weight of the rain that has now passed, a thin cloud of grey cigarette smoke pushed out in front of his face. He raises and lowers the pole to inspect his hooked bait before flicking it out across the surface again. He clears his throat and settles to watch once more, his shorn red head locked steady in concentration or contemplation, as if he is casting not for roach and perch but for memories and dreams.

The school is almost empty, the long corridors hollow as churches. The swarms of children are gone now for summer. In the silence of their wake I can still hear the clear tones of her voice moving about the painted walls, sliding beneath classroom doors, tapping upon the windowpanes.

17 Portnew

The Lambegs were starting as I made my way home, their urgent drumming following me along the Ways until I reached our street. My throat was dry, not with the heat of the day but with a kind of crying inside of me, a seizing in my chest.

Even when I closed my eyes as tight as I could, I couldn't keep out that picture of Raymond lapping up the white milk of Catherine's skin, her arms folded around his neck, pulling him down to her.

When I turned onto my street I saw Bingham's crew coming down Donald Lane and turning left into Simmons Street. The fortnight bunting was already up and Union Jacks hung from the windowsills, blue, red and white pansies fluttering in the window boxes. The fifes sang in unison now that the Cooke brothers had a few years of practise under their belts. Families stood at the gables of Simmons Street to welcome the marchers, hands clapping above their heads more in defiance than in any appreciation of the drums and fifes. Our street was empty, doors and windows locked shut against the din. A Land Rover was parked at the far end, its doors open, the officers lazing about in their shirtsleeves, saluting those they knew in the parade with a quietly clenched fist, a smile or a nod.

I slipped into the doorway of our house and watched the marchers turn the corner, pausing as they always did at the end of each Catholic terrace, the Lambegs beaten harder, the fifes rising ever higher. Bingham was suffering in the heat, his face turned a beetroot red, the metronomic beating of the sticks upon the skin counting his steps, kidney-shaped patches of sweat mottling his shirt and darkening the leather strap. Behind him was lifted the banner on its poles: the king on his prancing horse crossing the river, the silken letters of PORTNEW FAITH DEFENDERS stitched into a halo above his head.

I watched until they had turned into Simmons Street, where the noise suddenly dropped. The Land Rover revved and moved slowly off after them, leaving a cloud of diesel smoke between the kerbs of our street. Now the cheer that greeted the first march of the season would ripple its way down the ladder of terraces in the heat of the evening, kitchen chairs and upturned milk crates brought out to the pavements to enjoy the spectacle, pride and patriotism passed from street to street like an athlete's baton.

'Where have you been?' Ma was sitting at the kitchen table with the doors and windows closed to keep the noise of the marchers out. 'I seen you going out after breakfast was done and not a sign since.' She looked tired, the lines that had begun to show between her cheeks and nose more deeply etched now, the hair that was scraped back from her face to keep from sticking to her forehead in the heat making her look thin and severe. She leaned her head on her hand as I filled a glass from the tap. 'Well?'

'Just kicking about, Ma, that's all.'

'Aye?' she said, raising an eyebrow.

'Aye,' I firmed.

A chain whizzed in the back yard. Da was cleaning the bicycle again, stripped to the waist, an oily cloth flung over his shoulder, the bicycle upturned onto its saddle. Wasps circled about his head and he flicked the cloth to scatter them.

'And your sister?' Ma asked lazily.

'Catherine?' Something like panic started up inside me.

'Aye – I didn't think you had another.'

'Haven't seen her all day, Ma,' I managed.

'I don't see her these days at all. Where does she be going?' Ma was looking at the face of the old Bakelite radio that sat in a corner of the kitchen, the gold mesh screen in its centre that had begun to flake and crumble with age and damp, the station markings worn to nothing so that it had to be tuned by ear alone.

I said nothing in the hope that I could slip out to the back yard and Da and the pointless cleaning and polishing of the bicycle that masked the lack of work that was about.

'Well?' Ma didn't move her gaze from the old radio. Instead she squinted at it as if trying to make out the ghost etching of a station whose sound had once filled the room but had long since ceased to broadcast.

'Don't know, Ma,' I said quietly. 'I see her about the town though, at the arcades, the strand and that.'

'Hmm.' Ma curled her fingers through the handle of the empty mug that was before her. She scrubbed a hand into her hair and looked up at me. 'Your Da's in the yard,' she said, and smiled, knowing that I was anxious to be out of the kitchen and away from her questions.

As I went past her, with her bent back and bare neck with her hair fallen forward, I wanted to put a grip on her shoulder the way I'd seen Da do, to let her know that she was not alone in all of this. But she was my mother and I couldn't.

Da was going about the bike, tightening nuts and bolts with a spanner, pulling at stays and links to check for play.

I stood to watch him, my hands bunched in my pockets.

He straightened and pressed his fists into his sides and, as he stretched his back, he let out a groan. 'With the hot weather there'll be plenty will want their windows clean to get the best from it, and with the dust they'll need cleaning twice over,' he said, looking at me. 'Eh?'

I gave him a weak smile, and by the way he returned to the work on the bike I could tell that he knew I wouldn't be fooled. I watched him drawing a rag back and forth across the wheel rims that came up nickel-bright, his head nodding with the action, his legs braced against the bicycle frame so that it wouldn't topple over. He didn't speak again before I left the yard and all that time I wondered what he was thinking: the truth of things, or the same half-truths with which he had created a parallel world in which to hide.

Catherine didn't appear for dinner. Her untouched plate remained on the table long after the rest of us had finished, the cold meat attracting the attentions of two flies and a wasp that had come in from the yard. I shooed them out.

'Any sign?' Da asked when I stuck my head into the front room, where he was halfway through a bottle of Guinness. His shirt was open to the waist, the sunken chest and hollowed stomach patched with hairs that were turning grey. There were tight beads of sweat across his breastbone.

'No, Da, no sign.'

'She'll hear about it so when she gets back the night.' Da stared at the wall as if examining the tiny flowers in the wallpaper pattern that had paled to nothing in the light of years.

I went out to the doorstep to wait. I thought of going to look for her but I was afraid that I might find her with Raymond just as I had found them earlier on the railway embankment. I could never go back there. Ever.

I kicked a football about the back yard, waiting, not knowing what to do, caught between going to look for her and waiting to see what would happen when she did come back.

The beating of the Lambeg and the strains of the fifes were long gone, Bingham's party returning in the silence of exhaustion to their homes, white marching gloves peeled from their hands until the next march and the next, each one longer and slower than the one before until the finale on the Twelfth. Windows had been opened again on our street, net curtains sucked outwards to flutter like flags of peace or surrender.

Catherine never came back.

Da fell asleep over another bottle of Guinness, the

glass slumped between his legs and his arms fallen over the sides of the armchair. His snoring travelled the walls of the front room, passing across the faces of the living and the dead on the mantelpiece and the sideboard, and the purgatorial space between them, into which Catherine was to be pitched, neither dead nor alive, simply unknown.

Ma didn't sleep. I lay awake for a couple of hours after midnight listening to her moving about in her room. Sometimes she went to the window and looked down into the yard, where the hens could be heard roosting and a thousand wasps muttering in their nest of paper. There were long silences when I thought she might be sobbing, but then it would break and I'd hear the scratch of the bristles of a brush in her hair as she drew it out before the mirror, sweeping the hours of night before her.

'We'd best call the peelers,' Ma said in the morning. She was standing in Catherine's room, looking about her at the clothes heaped over the back of a chair, magazines scattered across the floor, the unmade bed. Ma gathered her arms across herself as if to stop the shaking that had taken hold. Her face was grey as ash.

'I'm minded to wait a wee while,' Da said. 'She could turn up any minute. Come on, son, we'll ask in the street.'

Da and I went along our street from house to house, calling on neighbours and asking after Catherine. None

Another Sky

remembered seeing her. None mentioned Raymond. We went around the shops and asked after her in the amusement arcades and the ice-cream parlours, which were just setting up for the day, canopies winched out tight, chillers thrumming into life. By the time we reached Ridge's at the end of the seafront we knew we weren't going to find her there. We wandered back to the Pillar Ballroom, where the dance floor was being mopped, the cavernous room cool as a church, our questions echoing around the walls. The cleaners leaned on their mops and shook their heads.

Ma was waiting at the front door when we returned, a clutch of neighbours gathered around her, their voices turned to whispers as we approached. 'Best call the peelers,' they advised.

Da set off to the station on his bike, his jacket thrown across the handlebars, the movement of his legs upon the pedals looking heavy and stiff with the weight of lead that was settling in his body and his heart.

An officer called to the house hours after Da had returned from the station, cursing the time they had left him waiting outside, their manner, the way nothing he had said was written down and how the desk sergeant had gone off to speak to the other officers and had not returned for twenty minutes.

'We're awful busy with the Twelfth,' the officer explained when Ma showed him through the door, 'and a young lad from across the town has gone

[167]

missing. There's a patrol looking for him and the coast-guard have been notified in case he went in off the shore. Raymond Harvey – his family have a shop on the Antrim road.'

While Da pulled a chair out for the officer I backed slowly out of the room. I stood in the hallway for what seemed a long, long time, listening to the officer's questions and the scratch of his pen across the pages of his day-book. Silent tears fell about my feet and onto the boards that Da had once so proudly and lovingly laid. The front door was still open and I could see people coming and going up and down the street, greeting each other with nods and winks, shopping bags slung over their arms. There was talk of the weather breaking. The sunlight was getting weaker, they said, the clouds beyond the quarry were black as night. The sea was gunmetal.

I ran up the stairs, Da's flats and risers flexing beneath my feet, and went into my room. There I found the display cases, the grids of wood and glass, the flotsam and jetsam of seasons past, the rows of eggs with their labels, summer after summer of them; all unanswering, innocent and illiterate.

18 Portnew

The cases are still there, furred with dust. The faded labels; yellow pigment thrown out like a shadow from the black Indian ink I had used to inscribe them. The neck of the bottle is charred with dried ink and the nib of the pen is so tarnished that the trade name has disappeared. The eggs lie perfectly still and penitent, stirring so many memories that I have to turn away to save myself from being overcome by them.

'Michael,' Ma calls from the kitchen below. 'There's tea if you want it.' Her voice seems too distant, as if it has come a long way inside her before it strikes the air. There is a frail resonance to it, like a torn drum.

'Aye, Ma. I'll be down now.'

I stop for a moment in the hallway before turning the handle to Catherine's room. When I open the door there is a smell that does not belong here, of citrus or wood or both. Her room has been cleared.

A few weeks after Catherine disappeared, Ma and a neighbour tidied her room, replacing the things the RUC officers had examined and returning her clothes to drawers and the wardrobe. Everything else was left as it was in preparation for the homecoming which has never happened. Sometimes, Ma would go in and sit on the edge of the bed, stock still, her hands fixed onto her knees so that she would not fold or break with crying. From there she could look out of the window and across the rows of chimney stacks and grey rooftops to where the sky seemed to thin out above the sea. Ma believed that Catherine was out there, somewhere, waiting to be found, waiting to come home.

Now the bed is made, a foot of white linen sheet folded back over a grey blanket. A pillow whose case has been worn gossamer-thin by the movement of skin and hair is plumped against the headboard. There is a great spareness to the room that reminds me of Frances's bedroom, an empty space at the heart of the house. A few books lean into each other on a shelf above the bed. An old porcelain shaving mug stops them from falling over. That smell I noticed is after-shave. Da sleeps here now.

The flats and risers have shrunk and the stairs creak as I go down. A few years ago Da and Ma had central heating put in when they got a grant for it. They keep the heat on most days now and everything has shrunk or warped in some way or another.

In the kitchen Ma is rinsing broccoli under the tap, the water drumming into the sink and skimming up her wrists like quicksilver.

'Is Da in Catherine's bedroom now, Ma?'

The tap keeps running and Ma continues to pass the broccoli florets beneath it, rinsing them almost until they begin to disintegrate.

'Ma?'

'Aye, he is.' She turns the tap off and shakes the colander so that water spatters onto the window. 'This long time now.' Her hair is a river of grey funnelling into a clasp above her neck, which is slack-skinned, the tendons gone loose and invisible. The tap squeaks shrilly like chalk on a blackboard when she tightens it. 'Your Da couldn't bear to hear me cry in the night when I'd wake thinking that your sister was still here and then remember that she was away. He couldn't reason with it. He said nothing, mind, but I could tell by the way he'd be watching me while I'd be getting his breakfast ready that he was hoping nothing would be said about it, and it never was. So here we are.'

She plunges the broccoli into a saucepan of water and sets it to boil, then sits down at the table with me, loosening her apron ties. I pour tea from the pot that has begun to cool.

'He was sleeping in your room for a few years and he'd move back in to sleep on the floor of ours whenever you'd come across to visit. We didn't want you to know.' She sighs and props her chin on her fist.

Her fingernails are bitten to raw skin. She had once been so proud of them, tiny glass jars of varnish and polish balanced on the arm of the armchair as she bent over each splayed finger in turn. Catherine used to want to blow them dry for her but she hushed her away, lying back to close her eyes as if to imagine that she was somewhere altogether more romantic and glamorous than one of the Portnew terraces.

'It's just, son,' she sighs, 'that we've spent all this time together and now we can't . . .'

'Aye,' I say.

'There's so much that we haven't said over the years, and now it's too late.' Ma traces a finger along the grain of the table as she speaks. Da's work: the grain still smooth after all these years, the countless teacups, plates and saucers. 'But we're getting on with life now – it gets easier the more you put things behind you.'

I think of everything that has happened and every-thing that must have gone unspoken in their lives, the centre hollowed out from within, like dry rot in a timber that looks perfect but can no longer bear weight.

'Well,' Ma says, getting up from the table. 'Those birds won't rest without feeding.'

'I'll do it, Ma.'

'Mind they don't nip you. You'll be a stranger to them now.'

Ma has taken to growing geraniums in the back yard and every ledge, nook and surface supports containers filled with geraniums. Some of Da's old galvanized buckets, their crimped seams crumbling with rust, swing from butcher's hooks nailed into the workshop eaves, geraniums trailing over their sides. A squall earlier in the day has scattered a multitude of petals across the grey cobbles like stamps fallen from a purse.

The bucket has a few inches of corn in it already, the sides streaked with scratches from the hens' beaks and claws when they leap to get at the grain. They come running when they see me with the bucket and I scatter the corn across their heads, sending it into every corner of the yard. Ma is watching me from the window, a grey ghost behind the glass, leaning on the taps. When I put down the bucket a pair of hens rush at it, tipping it over and scrambling inside. Ma is gone when I turn again towards the window to share a laugh with her.

The workshop has a new door and a new lock. The window has been cleaned. At my feet the cobbles are newly seamed with sawdust that has drifted there from beneath the workshop door.

'There you are, Michael!' Da calls out as he comes under the arch, wheeling the bicycle, his trousers tucked into his socks even though he no longer cycles and only pushes the bicycle about the town. 'We were beginning to wonder if you were going to pay us a visit at all this summer – if summer you want to call it,' he says, glancing up at the sky, which is cut to blue ribbons by cloud, the slate roofs still mottled with wet from the morning squall.

When he takes my shoulder in greeting he squeezes it again and again while we talk, as if he is looking for something in me. His grip is weaker now, the mechanics unsure of themselves.

He asks the same questions about my life in London that he has always asked. Do I see many others from Northern Ireland? Am I happy sharing the flat with other lads? Would I be bringing a young lassie back one of these days and settling down with a family of my own? He had always made a joke of this last question, but because he always asked it I knew that it bothered him that I was already at an age when he himself had been married with two children.

He leans the bicycle against the downpipe, where his buckets hang, dusted with tarnish, the wiper blades split from neglect and disuse. He washes few windows now.

'Was it the boat or the plane you came across on?'

'The plane, Da.'

'You like your comforts well enough.' He smiles.

Boat or plane would always end with the Ulsterbus from Larne or Aldergrove. Ballymena, Portglenone,

Kilrea, Milltown, the towns and villages ticked off one by one, Orange towns, Republican towns, some with their hearts blown out one Christmas and rebuilt the next, some not rebuilt at all, and always the Bann sliding so slowly by to my left or right, thoughts and memories carried out to sea.

'Da?' I ask, shuffling at the fresh sawdust with the toe of my shoe.

'Oh, aye,' he says, looking down. A thin smile breaks on his lips and instantly he seems to shed some of the years that hang heavily upon his frame. He searches in his pockets. 'Let me show you something, son,' he says eventually, a key glimmering in the palm of his hand.

When he opens the workshop door it is as if a lifetime's worth of memories are carried out on that musky smell of wood. We stand there recognizing and acknowledging the moment before he shows me inside.

Little of what I remember is left. The loft where Catherine hid has been dismantled and the joists from which it hung are covered with sheets of plasterboard. The great deal bench with its row of vice grips and circular saw is gone too, a pair of folding workbenches in its place. Only the Coronet lathe remains.

'Don't bother,' Da says when I try to switch it on. 'It's eaten out with rust. It was left for so long that the bearings are shot altogether.'

When I run my hand across the enamelled metal

casing and Coronet badge I imagine it springing to life like it used to, as vibrant as something living.

'Come here, Michael,' Da says, ushering me across to the trestle table pushed up against the window.

'What's that, Da?' An old sheet is draped over a large box-shaped object that is sitting there.

Da smiles and carefully lifts the sheet to reveal a wooden doll's house whose rooms and hallways are filled with miniature furniture, the doors perfect in their panelled detail, wall mirrors the size of finger-nails. Even the hinged roof is covered with carved tiles that are so small they might be the scales of fish.

'There's a couple of rooms to finish yet, but it's almost there. To my mind it's the best work I've ever done, Michael. Only a couple of hours a day, but a couple of very good hours all the same.' He fingers a row of small chisels whose blades look impossibly narrow. 'What do you think?'

'It's amazing, Da,' I say, peering through the front door and along a hallway that is no wider than my hand. A row of empty picture frames hangs on the wall.

I remember the houses that Frances and I would pass on our walks home in London the summer before, the lit windows and clean rooms arranged like a series of still lifes.

19 London

We found each other again, or rather, she found me.

There she was, sitting on my doorstep, when I returned from school on the first day of the new term. Her arms were folded across her drawn-up knees, from which the pleats of her skirt fell perfectly to her ankles. Her hair shone, tucked behind her ears. I stood looking at her for a few moments, thinking of all the things I wanted to say.

We sat side by side on the step for a long time, not touching, not speaking, just watching cars pass up and down the road and people coming home from work. The evenings were beginning to grow cold then and the first leaves were already falling, twisting through the air above our heads. Swallows were working the back gardens and the skies beyond the rooftops. I made a pot of tea and brought it out onto the steps. I watched her blow on the tea when she cupped the mug in her hands. That was enough for me.

'Where did you go?' I said.

'I sold the flat.'

'I know.'

'I went home to stay with my mother for the summer. I taught English to Spanish students until I could bear it no longer.'

'The students? The teaching?'

'My mother,' she sighed. 'We're too alike. We want things to be perfect, to have it all worked out in advance so that nothing can go wrong. Of course, they always do.'

'Always?'

'Well, not always. Sometimes it just looks that way.'

While we talked the sun sank behind the houses to leave an orange glow in the tops of the trees that lined the road. It grew cold on the steps and Frances drew her arms around her.

'So I came back here. I stayed with friends in Tooting and did absolutely nothing for a few weeks. It felt great, just great.'

'And here you are,' I said.

'Yes, here I am,' she said, looking into my face.

I put my arm around her and pulled her close. She bent her head. My fingers traced the faint ridges of goose pimples across her elbow.

'Another week and you wouldn't have found me.' I smiled, nodding at the house behind us. 'They're about to gut the place. I'm the only one left.'

'So we have it to ourselves, then?'

'Aye. For a few days anyway.'

They were wonderful, those few days of summer slipping into autumn. More wonderful, perhaps, because in this new beginning was the ending of our old lives.

The house continued to fall down around us. The iron bath cracked so we took to washing each other on the floor of the kitchen, just standing there sponging each other with the rivers of water finding their way through the floorboards and under the skirtings. We didn't care. We cared only for each other and the love-making we knew would come amidst the garlands of soap. Afterwards, we would eat in one of the local restaurants, lingering for the last hour over a bottle of wine before returning to the house and our bed, where we talked almost until dawn.

Each morning I rose for school at eight, unlocking my limbs from hers and leaving without waking her, the wonder of her hair splayed across the pillows, her clothes on hangers in the wardrobe. I could hardly believe she was there.

On our last evening in the house I showed her the

pebble I had taken from her flat during the estate agent's tour.

'It's yours,' I said.

'You keep it,' she said, and smiled, folding my fingers back over it.

20 Portnew

There are so many empty houses here now, blocked
windows looking out on empty streets, buddleia and
dandelion sprouting unchecked from the seams of their
walls and foundations. Glennon's house at the end of
our terrace is long-since sealed, the brickwork hazed
with graffiti both new and old, a Red Hand daubed on
the gable that looks towards Simmons Street, Tri-
colours painted in the blocked windows along ours.
I remember how almost everyone in our street had
squeezed into Glennon's front room to watch Mary
Peters in the Olympics and how I had to stand on their
windowsill to get a proper view of the television screen.
Glennon's front door has disappeared behind a steel
grille and layers of daubed paint, but the stub of what
was once the only television aerial in our street
remains, rusted to the chimney stack.

I pause when I pass the entrance to the Ways. The

sounds of boys playing carries along the cracked concrete, their voices high, shouting, yelping, the scuff of their shoes on the ground.

A clutch of girls is sitting on the sea wall and looking out at the sea, which is changing from green to grey and back again as clouds move across it. Their legs swing in tandem while they talk and they pull hair away from their faces again and again.

The breeze is gathering waves and flattening them against the sand, ribbons of foam pushed up in ridges at the tide line, where broken razor and cockle shells have been dredged.

When I hear the whoops and calls of the surfers I look up and see three of them, rising onto their boards, which are lifting up on a wave, dark shapes against the silvered horizon, their arms searching for balance, bending at the knee, looking always as if they are about to jump. The wind tugs at their voices so that they come to me like fragments of another language, preverbal, broken syllables and yelps that might be seagulls circling far overhead.

I walk to the end of the strand, to where the sand thickens with rocks and flotsam, scraps of fishing net, plastic bottles, wood that has been aged by the oceans, seaweed of every colour. A dogfish has been cast up on the tide line, a shark in miniature, the spotted flanks and the belly that is perfectly smooth and pale as a woman's skin.

Frances is at home in our London flat now. I wanted her to come with me to announce our engagement, but she wouldn't. She teaches English to Japanese businessmen working in the City and they have exams at the end of the week. They call her for advice and to check their pronunciation with her. She doesn't want to let them down by not being there.

From here at the end of the strand the town could be anywhere. So perfectly is it hunched between the gnawed face of the quarry and the strand that the decay of its streets is hidden from view, row after row of rooftops interrupted only by a few church spires. The hotels and guesthouses that line the promenade have been repainted in bright colours, flags snapping in their gardens, window boxes filled with petunias and lobelia. Ridge's ice-cream parlour is now a surfer's café, haunted by men whose bleached hair hangs in ponytails down their necks and whose shorts reach to their knees.

Portnew is a different place now. Whole families have left, moved across the border or the sea to new cities and new lives, some never to return. The cement works is long since closed and the train brings but a few visitors now that so many people have cars. The shopping streets have been cobble-locked and pedestrianized, and violas and sweet williams flutter happily in half-barrels on street corners.

I can hardly bear to come back. Everything I have

known here has moved away from me in small, almost imperceptible movements, like the tide when you're not looking.

And Catherine. Somewhere, long after she disappeared, she stopped being a part of my life, so that now she lives on in scattered fragments and half-forgotten histories, a legacy of the childhood we shared together.

It is in the rain of Portnew that I will always see her, a hood pulled down over her eyes, drops clinging to the fringe, bare legs half blue beneath a cotton skirt. There is nothing to hide the silken skin that rainwater beads upon, the dark hair, the green eyes, the broken mouth, the quick and mischievous smile, the smooth limbs of a princess. Time has not dimmed her, but with each memory she is taken further from me, smaller and smaller, so that she is summoned, still perfect but with greater effort.